Rumer

by

Angela Kay Austin

Vanilla Heart Publishing
USA

Rumer

by Angela Kay Austin

Copyright 2013 Angela Kay Austin

Published by: Vanilla Heart Publishing
www.VanillaHeartBooksAndAuthors.com
10121 Evergreen Way, 25-156
Everett, WA 98204 USA

This book is a work of fiction. Names, characters, places, and incidents are either the product of the author's imagination or are used fictitiously, and any resemblance to places, events, or persons living or dead is purely coincidental.

ISBN: 978-061597-70-10

10 9 8 7 6 5 4 3 2 1 First Edition

First Printing, February 2014
Printed in the United States of America

Rumer

by

Angela Kay Austin

Table of Contents

Dedication and Acknowledgements

Chapter One... 13
Chapter Two... 21
Chapter Three... 27
Chapter Four... 33
Chapter Five... 39
Chapter Six... 45
Chapter Seven... 51
Chapter Eight... 55
Chapter Nine... 59
Chapter Ten... 63
Chapter Eleven... 69
Chapter Twelve... 73
Chapter Thirteeen... 79
Chapter Fourteen... 85
Chapter Fifteen... 91
Chapter Sixteen... 101
Chapter Seventeen... 107
Chapter Eighteen... 111
Chapter Nineteen... 121
Chapter Twenty... 129
Chapter Twenty-One... 137
Chapter Twenty-Two... 143
Chapter Twenty-Three... 151
Chapter Twenty-Four... 157
Chapter Twenty-Five... 165
Chapter Twenty-Six... 175
Epilogue... 183

Book Club Discussion Guide
More Great Books by Angela Kay Austin
Angela Kay Austin Author Bio and Photo

Dedication

To everyone who has ever been afraid
to allow themselves to love.

Acknowledgements

When you find that one special person who makes you catch your breath every time they say your name, you hope that feeling will never end. But, sometimes, it does. That doesn't mean you'll never feel that "special" feeling again.

I've witnessed many people I love find love, lose love, and find love again. Their strength and ability to continue forward with their lives and open their hearts to love again is what inspired this book.

Chapter One

Rumer Wilson glanced over her shoulder, again, at the woman silently waiting and watching her and her two children from the end of the line. From fresh produce to milk, the woman had been on every aisle. Although the dark haired brown eyed woman looked familiar, she was confident she didn't know her. If she were a member of one of her charity organizations, congregation, or someone she'd helped in the past, she'd remember. Again, she surveyed the woman – bronzed skin, taller, deep waves of curls covering her shoulders ending at a bust that was much more ample than her own small breasts. Her long legs were lengthened even more by the height of her strappy sandals. Rumer couldn't remember the last time she'd worn her own hair in curls, or worn sandals, either. You can't run after a three year-old in strappy summer sandals, unless you wanted a twisted ankle.

Rumer paid quickly, stuffing the money the cashier handed her carelessly into her purse, and then sped around the check-out counter to catch her runaway three year-old. "Madison, come back here." Rumer Wilson's voice was soft, but firm. Her daughter stopped where she stood, and peered over her shoulder briefly before she shot toward the doors which led to the vestibule of the grocery store.

Rumer pushed her overloaded shopping cart, which held her six month-old son safely in his carrier, toward the doors. The cuff of her sleeve served as a wipe when she dabbled at milky drool oozing from the corner of his mouth. "Madison," she yelled again when she realized her daughter used that quick moment to run again.

The bagger at a nearby register noticed her desperation, and snagged her scampering daughter by the arm before she could escape through the doors. "Here you are Ma'am," he said. The stocky blond released her daughter's arm as she reached for her.

Relief flooded her as she met the young man's metallic smile with her own. "Thank you so much." Rumer tightly held Madison's hand, and walked into the vestibule. She squatted so that she and the tiny runaway were on the same level. "Maddie, you know you are supposed to hold onto Mommy's cart when we are in the grocery store."

Madison's eyes averted Rumer's. She twisted a long black plait around a tiny finger. "Yes, Mommy."

"Do not run like that again." With one hand on her cart, and the other holding Madison's, she crossed the parking lot of the grocery store, slowly, in search of her car, allowing the hot sun to chase away the chill from the to-cold store. When she reached the car, she no longer felt the need to wrap her arms around herself for warmth or check Ty's blankets to ensure he was comfortable. She was sure Maddie had been fine because she ran up and down the aisles. What better way to stay warm?

Rumer buckled and belted both children into their carseats in the backseat, then lowered the windows, and popped the trunk. Strategically, she loaded bag after bag.

"Excuse me, Mrs. Wilson?" the voice asked with a question.

Startled, Rumer bumped her head on the inside hood of her trunk as she stood and stepped back to see who was calling her name. She rubbed a hand over the tender spot on the back of her head. "Yes?" Surprise colored her word. The voice did not fit the body; it was slightly lower than she expected. The woman from the end of the line—up close, she was even more beautiful. Meticulously plucked eyebrows enhanced flawless make-up which seemed unnecessary because of her beautiful creamy skin. "Can I help you?"

"Ma'am, I don't mean to cause you any harm, but I think you should know—"

Rumer was confident she did not know this woman. And although the woman seemed nice enough, she didn't have a lot of time before the kids would become agitated by their seatbelts. She cut off the woman's words. "Are you sure you want me?"

"Yes, Ma'am. You are Mrs. Wilson. Mrs. Luke Wilson?"

"Yes, that's me."

The person in front of her handed her a handful of papers. Rumer's eyes scanned the familiar handwriting that filled the pages she held. The words were beautiful. The person who'd written them had made the decision to end the relationship. She could feel the man's heartache. Although he loved the woman who, according to the letters, filled his dreams and clouded his judgment, he couldn't leave his wife and children. He had too much to lose.The letters were signed with a single "L."

Rumer stared into the glassy eyes of the beautiful woman standing in front of her. No one wrote letters...except her husband. He hand wrote "thank you" cards, notes to friends, anything. According to him, everyone was forgetting about the personal touch. Her eyes fell back to the letters she held. She traced every curve and slant with her eyes. Love letters. Love letters from her husband, Luke, to the woman in front of her.

"Mrs. Wilson, I knew you might not believe me, so I thought I would do better by showing you. For months, we've been seeing each other."

Rumer wasn't listening. She shuffled through the pages in her hands, scanning as quickly as her eyes would move, taking in as much as her brain could process. Ten years of marriage, two children, and a life built together. This couldn't be real.

It has to be a lie.

Was this a member of the church she didn't remember that was upset with her or Luke? Why would this woman do this now? Do it here with her children less than two feet away.

She shook the papers at the woman, and then ripped them in half

"Mommy...Mommy," Madison cried.

RUMER

Tyler joined in and wailed with her.

Rumer wiped away the tears on her own face; she inhaled deeply, and walked to Tyler's window. She kissed him on the cheek, and rubbed his stomach. His cries turned into sniffles until they disappeared. She looked over at Madison. "Maddie, it's okay. Mommy will be right back." If she didn't know better, she'd swear Maddie knew her heart ached. Her daughter's beautiful dark eyes questioned her before she sniffed and rubbed the back of her hand across her eyes. Rumer took that moment to look away. Her glare returned to the woman standing beside the rear of her car.

"Mrs. Wilson, I'm only here to let you know. I told him I would tell you if he didn't. I never wanted this."

Rumer whispered sternly, "What do you mean? He's a deacon. He's married." Rumer pointed at the backseat of her car. "Those are his children." Cautiously, she neared the woman.

"I met him at a center I go to sometimes." Her eyes strayed away. "He volunteered at the center. I told him I had developed feelings, and he broke things off."

The face of the woman in front of her showed sincerity and pain. But, no trace of deceit. She wanted to hate her, to punch her. What this woman told her would change her whole world.

It would destroy her family.

"After some time passed, he found me, and told me he thought he had feelings for me, but that it wouldn't work." She nodded toward the back seat of the car, and then at Rumer. "Because of the children, you, his work, and the church."

Rumer did not want to hear anymore. She'd heard all she needed. "So, why are you here?"

"Because," she hesitated before continuing, "none of us are happy like this. He and I want to be together, but he's afraid. I've dealt with all of this before, but he hasn't."

She's dealt with it all before? Did she make a habit of finding married men to sleep with, and ruin their marriages?

Rumer leaned her butt against one of her taillights. Her legs didn't feel like they could hold her. She took in everything about the woman. The only place he'd volunteered, lately, was with the LGBT center. He'd seen something on the news about a need for funding and attacks, and wanted to get involved. He'd lost his own brother because of bullying and couldn't stand to see others going through the same thing.

Rumer sucked in her breath as she processed what the woman in front of her just said. Her heartbeat could barely be controlled by her breathing because her mind rolled the acronym over in her head. LGBT—lesbians, gays, bisexuals, and transgendered. Her arms trembled as she braced herself against the trunk of the car.

The woman reached for her, but stopped. Good thing, too. Rumer didn't know how she'd respond. It took all her strength not to scream and hit.

The woman waved her hands up and down her body. Rumer followed her manicured hands from the top of her gorgeous brunette head, to her impeccably applied make-up, to her breasts, to her flat stomach, to her white capris that showed off toned calves, and finished with her French manicured toes.

"I am very open about who I am. It's hard, but it's who I am. When I realized how I felt about him, I told him. He didn't know."

Who was she? Is she a he? Rumer let her eyes roam the woman again. She had breasts, and it didn't look like she had a penis. She squinted to look harder until she thought it was just stupid.

"How many months?" Rumer braced herself for the response.

"Several, but...our relationship isn't sexual. We talk, we go for walks, and we share each other's company." She paused. "That's why he didn't know."

Know what? She must be a he! If she was "open" about herself, why wasn't that the first thing she told him?

RUMER

Rumer didn't want to hear her reasons why. Her excuses. He was a married man. Her husband. "Why wasn't it the first thing you told him?"

"I don't know..." she said, softly. "It's not how I live my life. But, for the first time in a long time, I felt 'normal' with him. With him," she paused, "I felt like a regular woman spending time with a man." She stopped and waited.

Rumer knew too well how Luke could make you feel like you were the only woman in the universe. He'd done that with her from the day they'd first met. Only recently had she felt the unexplainable change. She'd chalked it up to work or stress. As she stared at the woman in front of her, she began to stitch the pieces together.

"How did you find me?" Rumer asked.

"I found your church, and then I found you."

"I don't...I don't know what..." Rumer couldn't finish her sentence because she didn't know what she wanted to say.

"I just thought you should know. I don't see him anymore, but I thought you should know. I work and live in Glen Burnie, Maryland. Everyone calls me Gabriela. If you want to talk you can reach me through my job at the nail salon called Elite Nails."

Rumer watched Gabriela walk away, and then she stared at the wad of wrinkled, tear-stained papers in her hand. She loaded the remaining bags of groceries into the trunk, closed it, and drove her children home. Not even the lavender scented car freshener Luke bought her helped her calm down. She lowered her car window, ripped the thing from her vent and tossed it out of the car.

Baths were given. She read Maddie her favorite bedtime story, and turned on Tyler's musical dancing lights. She showered, and then put on her pajamas.

Then she stopped. She stood in front of the mirror hanging on the back of her closet door, and she stared at herself. Next to Gabriela, she looked like a man. It had been six months since Tyler was born. She hadn't lost the baby weight, yet, and it showed in her round hips and belly. She hadn't done anything to her hair. She cut it and wore it in a pony-tail most of the time. She never wore make-up, and she couldn't remember the last time she'd been to a spa for anything. Who had the time? She was a full-time mom—cook, maid, chauffeur, butler, teacher, and nurse.

Tugging at her stained blue flannel pajamas with little yellow ducks, she wondered if any man would think they were sexy. They were a gift Luke and Maddie had bought her for Mother's Day, and they were comfy. Hurriedly, she tore them off, and searched through her dresser for something silky and more grown up. The only thing she could find was a black full slip she would normally wear to church under one of her dresses.

Rumer assessed herself again, and thought *much better*. The black slip had thicker bra-like straps, but the silky fabric flowed softly over her breasts and hips. It had a little split on the right side, and a little strip of lace encircled the hem. She sprayed a little cucumber melon body spray on her skin; turned the radio on to one of her favorite jazz stations, and lit some vanilla scented candles. Then she focused on the bed. Snatching at the covers, she searched through the linen closet for the black satin sheets that she knew were there somewhere.

They'd never used them.

She waited in bed propped up by black satin covered pillows, and waited for her husband to come home.

At 11:30 P.M., she heard the chime of the alarm system. Luke walked down the hall to Maddie's room, then to Tyler's, and finally he came to their room. She couldn't hear his footsteps, but she knew his routine. The same thing every night.

Rumer sprang from bed, and bounced into her husband's arms. She wrapped her arms around his neck, and attempted to kiss him.

He kissed her on the cheek before pushing her away. "I'm tired. I had a long day at work and then I had to drop by the church, too. I really want to go to sleep."

RUMER

She retreated at his rejection. Pulling at the bottom of her slip, she tried to stretch it to cover the rest of her body, but it wouldn't budge. The lace at the bottom ripped. She grabbed her fluffy robe from the walk-in closet, and stood there in the closet doorway, watching as Luke undressed to his boxers, prayed, and then climbed into bed and covered himself with the covers.

He buried his face in the pillows, and conceded an unintelligible, "Good night."

"Good night." Rumer left the room, and padded barefoot down the carpeted hallway to the laundry room. Instantly, the overpowering smell of detergent and fabric softener flooded her senses. The chill of the tiled laundry room floor cooled her feet. She reached into the wooden cabinet behind the laundry detergent, and removed the letters Gabriela had given her. Leaning against the dryer with the pages crushed to her heart, she sobbed.

Rumer cried until she had no more tears to shed.

She checked on her son, and then walked into her daughter's room where she curled up next to her on her tiny twin bed and prayed, "Give me the strength."

She closed her eyes, and drifted off to sleep. Maybe it was all a dream.

Chapter Two

Rumer sat on the edge of the bed, and took off her black sandals. Book club was her one "Mommy only" outing every month, and she loved it. But, now she probably only had a few minutes before Maddie would come storming into her room or before Tyler began to cry. The bed squeaked as she leaned back. They really needed a new mattress, even if they didn't use it for anything but sleeping. They'd had the set, in fact, she scanned the room, they'd owned everything in it since the first year of their marriage. She stripped out of her jeans and blouse, and then placed her jewelry into the jewelry box her grandmother had given her, where it sat on the top of the dresser.

She tugged on her comfy gray sweats and flip-flops, and then she trudged down the hall toward the family room. The children were awfully quiet, and she wanted to know what was going on before she started dinner.

She stopped at Luke's office door, and poked her head through the doorway. "Hey, honey, do you need anything?"

He didn't look up from his computer. "No."

"Are you hungry at all?"

He lifted his head from his computer. A wary smile curved his lips. She hadn't seen him smile in awhile. Weekends always seemed to make him happy, at least the ones he worked at the center, when she really thought about it. She dropped the thought and refocused her eyes on him. She couldn't take them off him. He had beautiful features – chiseled cheeks, straight white teeth, dark skin, and bald head. Since college, she'd loved him from the day she met him. He'd done everything he could to catch her attention.

RUMER

And when he had it, he'd promised to love her forever. He lied!

"Would you mind making some of your delicious spaghetti?" His head bowed back to the computer screen. Lately, he spent more time hunched over his computer than he did doing anything else. Not really typing. She couldn't really remember hearing the sound of the keyboard much. So maybe, what he was doing was reading.

"Sure." Something she didn't want to acknowledge nagged at her as she dragged herself away from the room and headed down the hallway to the children.

Tyler was sleeping, and Maddie was coloring something on the floor. Great. She'd have to clean that up before it set in the carpet. She didn't feel like dealing with it today. Maybe tomorrow.

While Rumer prepared dinner she thought about the book her book club discussed—*"Man in the Making"*. The author was a man who'd written the book for his sons. He said there were three steps: availability, communication, and commitment. Every woman in the book club had their own idea about what that meant. The author had his interpretation, but it was written by a man for men. How did it fit for a woman? Of the seven members of her book club: three were married, three single – two because of divorce and one never married – and one lived with her boyfriend. They all thought they'd made themselves available, and who communicated better than women, no one. Commitment— that one got the conversation going. Everyone had a different meaning for the word commitment, and how infidelity should be treated.

Until now, she never thought she'd be one of those women who accepted any version of infidelity regardless of how big or small. But, that was because she never thought she'd have to deal with it.

Dinner was filled with catering to the kids, tamping down her fear, and nurturing her hate for Gabriela.

After putting her children to bed, she joined Luke in their bedroom. He was still awake. He threw the covers up so she could join him. Soft kisses and tender caresses lulled her body into his. Pleasant and gentle. That's how she'd describe their love-making. Not thunderous and head-banging, but sweet. But, there were those rare nights when...she didn't know what got into him, but whatever it was, she liked it. She wished they had more of those nights.

Tonight wasn't one of them.

Luke rolled over onto his side—away from her, and she wrapped herself around him. Her eyes closed, and she drifted off to sleep.

Rumer's eyes opened as her brain woke from its sleepy fog. She didn't know how many hours had passed, but she heard his snores from the pillow behind her. Quietly, she rose from bed, and silently sneaked down the hallway to his office. Her heart pounded. With each step and motion it thumped harder. She could feel it in her ears. The sound of the computer's fan echoed through the quiet house. She keyed in the password, and waited. Once the computer finished loading email, she began. Email after email confirmed everything Gabriela had said was true. Their conversations had begun simple enough. Then, over time, the emails became more and more personal for both of them. His emails never said he was unhappy with her, but he felt something was missing, and he didn't know what because he'd loved Rumer for so long. In his opinion, only a man with a weak will would cheat, and leave his family.

But, even if he hadn't left his family, he'd still strayed.

Did he think he was weak? Did she?

Rumer shut the computer off. She'd seen enough.

She snuck back into their bedroom, and into their bed.

When she awoke the next morning, Luke was gone. He always went to work early on Mondays because he wanted to have longer hours at the center.

Now, she knew the real reason why.

She packed her ten-year old luggage—a wedding gift, and then she loaded up Maddie's Dora the Explorer pack, and Tyler's diaper bag. She loaded everyone and everything into her minivan, and backed out of the overstuffed two-car garage. As she rolled backwards, she let her eyes scan the littered history of her marriage: tricycle, Christmas tree, and winter clothes... she left it all behind.

She didn't know if she'd ever see any of it again.

Rumer didn't quite know what would happen when Luke returned home to read her note? He might try to take her children. How could she fight him? She hadn't worked since becoming a mother. What daycare would Maddie attend? Would she be able to afford it? Would she get alimony and child support?

Rumer didn't cry. Crying never solved her problems. She drove. There was only one place for her to go.

Rush hour traffic always sucked, but the three-hour drive to Hampton, Virginia was quiet, otherwise. Tyler slept, and Maddie busied herself coloring, and pushing buttons on her fake telephone. She pulled into the driveway of the small familiar home, and came to a slow stop. She'd called Grandma Mae during her trip to let her know she and the kids would be there, but she didn't tell her why. Lying to her grandmother hadn't been her intention, but what was she supposed to tell her? *Grandma, I think Luke is in love with another woman. And, oh yeah, she's not all woman—physically.*

She could hear her grandmother's voice in her head, scolding her. Telling her what she and Luke needed to do. How they needed to think about their children and his career. But, what was she supposed to do?

I can't change who Luke loves.

The only thing she could do was hold onto the little bit of dignity she had, find a job, and take care of her children. Reaching up to adjust the rearview mirror, she watched as Tyler slept. Tears she'd held back for days stung her eyes, but she fought them back.

Maddie spoke, "Mommy. You sad?"

She glanced at her daughter who watched her with wide innocent eyes. Sad. It barely covered the emotions Rumer kept bottled inside. "Tired, sweetie. We had a long drive."

Her daughter's prying eyes didn't stop their inquisition, but as if she knew she wouldn't get another answer, she said, "I'm hungry, Mommy. Can I get out?"

Rumer popped the locks, and opened her car door. "Yes, baby. I'll help you out, now." As she exited the car, her grandmother stepped onto the front porch. Mae Brown's long dark hair and fair complexion hinted to her ancestry, a mixture of white, Native American, and black. Her thin frame was both a product of long morning walks and age. Rumer's complexion mirrored her mothers, and so did Tyler's, but as she glanced into the backseat at Maddie, she marveled at how much her daughter reminded her of her grandmother.

Rumer's grandmother had practically raised her after her mother lost her battle with breast cancer. Her father hadn't been the most reliable man, and after he remarried, he moved to the west coast, quickly forgetting he had a daughter. According to Grandma Mae, he couldn't face Rumer because she reminded him too much of her mother. A woman he'd loved too long and too hard to say good bye to. But, none of it mattered to Rumer because no matter how you looked at it, she didn't have a father or mother.

Grandma Mae lifted her long skirt just slightly so that she could walk down the steps of the porch and, as soon as she could, she embraced Rumer. She smelled like syrup. Not the strawberry or blueberry kind you see in restaurants, but the old fashioned maple syrup. Her soft hair brushed against Rumer's cheek as she pulled away. Memories of her childhood flooded her mind. How many times had she felt that same thing? Too many times, she'd tangled her fingers in her grandmother's hair as she'd cried on her shoulder about everything from boys to not fitting in at college. Now, as she released her grandma from her embrace, she wished so hard she didn't have to. Her grandmother's love and warmth flowed right through every pore of her body refueling her. That brief contact gave her the energy she needed to step away and release her grandmother from her bear hug. If she held on any longer, it would be a dead giveaway that something was wrong. She could never keep secrets from her, and if she broke down in tears that would be a huge clue.

"I'm so happy you guys are here." She reached out and squeezed Rumer's arms as she spoke. "Seeing you and the

25

family at the holidays isn't enough." Then, she pushed by her and headed for the backseat of the car.

Before Rumer could get Tyler, grandma Mae had began to unbuckle him, and lift him from his chair. He squirmed and opened his eyes. At first, Rumer thought he would protest and she waited for his piercing cries, but when grandma kissed him on the cheek, and stroked her hand along his leg, his large doe eyes brightened, and he gurgled. Amazing how spit bubbles can be cute. Grandma Mae always had a magic touch when it came to Tyler. If anyone else had disturbed his sleep, including her, he'd let you know he didn't like, loudly.

"Mommy," Maddie grunted as she pulled at her seat belt. "Help."

She rounded the car, and assisted her three-year old. The little girl was all smiles as soon as her feet hit the ground. She ran around the car, and hugged Grandma Mae's legs.

"Ganny, I'm hungry."

Grandma Mae loved those words. Find a seventy year-old woman in the south who didn't pride herself on her cooking prowess. Rumer watched a smile bloom on her grandmother's face, as she said, "Well, then, why don't we all go inside, and have a little breakfast. Rumer, we can empty the car later." She turned to walk back towards the house with Rumer following. "Catch me up on what you have been doing. How's Luke?"

"We haven't been doing much. Luke's fine," she lied. Grandma Mae dragged her attention away from Tyler and stared at Rumer, but Tyler's coos saved her. Grandma nuzzled his belly with her nose, and forgot about her, for the moment.

That was the first lie she'd told her grandmother since she was a teenager sneaking out for a date with a guy from school that her grandmother didn't like. How many more times would she lie? How many more people would she have to lie to? Lots of people divorced. Every day.

Chapter Three

What happened after feeding and bathing the children was nothing but a blur to Rumer. Maybe the ride had taken more out her than she thought, but no matter the reason, as she stretched out her body it cracked and popped in subtle protest. She'd love to snuggle back into the covers beside Luke and forget.

She closed her eyes, and pretended that he was the one cooking eggs and bacon for breakfast. Inhaling long and deep, she opened her eyes as she exhaled and flung the covers away from her body. Swinging her legs over the side of the tiny day bed, she forced herself to shake the silly thoughts out of her head. Wouldn't it be wonderful if everything she knew was not true, but that just wasn't the case, was it?

At that thought, she snatched her phone from the small wooden table next to the bed, and saw she had several missed calls from Luke. As she scrolled down the call log an odd feeling of something being right in the universe washed over her. Hope. She admitted to herself as it faded. She'd left the note telling him where she was going, but no explanation.

Was it really necessary?

She hit the button to play her voicemail, and braced herself. But, no, he wasn't angry. Voicemail after voicemail, his voice sounded scared. She didn't know if it was for her, him, or their children. But, the well-thought out slowly spoken messages weren't what she expected. He was never a mean person, but he was extremely confident in all things. The pleas into her voicemail weren't ordinary for him. Not at all.

She took the chance, and called him.

"Rumer," he answered with a hint of nervousness.

"Luke, the kids are okay." She knew he'd be concerned. Because no matter what, he was still their father.

"Rumer...I—"

"You should've told me." The anger she'd hidden from everyone, including herself boiled. "Your 'friend' followed me to the grocery store." She paused. "I was with the children. They were scared and crying."

"Can we talk about this when you get back home?" he asked.

"You don't want to talk about your children being afraid or about your 'friend.'" He owed her an explanation. They'd been married for ten years. Ten years of her catering to him and his career. Ten years of her putting herself last. Three of those ten she'd cared not only for him, but for their children. And he thinks he can sweep it all under a rug and forget about it. "Why?"

"Baby, I'm your husband. We're married." There was a pause on his phone line. "I'm sorry about what happened. I promise. It will never happen again." Another pause on the line. "If you need to spend some time there with your grandmother, okay. But, please, come back home."

"Luke, I'm not sure I'm coming back home. Why?" She pressed the issue. "I can't give you what you want."

"What does that mean?"

Her words had sparked something that angered him. The calm tones of his voice were fading.

"Gabriela is a 'he,' right?" She ran a hand down the length of her body as she sat on the side of the bed. "At least part of her is or was."

"I didn't have sex with a man," he stated. "I worked with her. She developed feelings for me."

"And what about you?" she asked.

"You are my wife and I'm your husband." He paused. "I don't know what I'm going to have to do to convince you that I'll do anything to keep my family." The word family faded before he finished saying it. "I'll give you some time to think." He hung up the phone.

She still had the phone in her hand when it rang again. "Luke, I don't want to talk if you're just going to say what you want and hang up on me."

"Rumer, I'm sorry. I'm not..." his voice softened, "...gay." He paused. "I don't want to talk about this."

"Luke, we have to talk about this. I need to know what's going on with you. With us." What did he expect from her? For her to just let it be. For her to not ask questions, and do what he said, like a good little girl.

"You come home and we can talk," he said.

"I don't know, Luke. I think we should talk while I'm here, and you're there." She hoped he wouldn't be able to easily fool her when he was two hundred miles away. Maybe she'd be able to see him for the man he truly was, and not the man she'd wanted him to be. There wouldn't be the temptation of his kiss or touch, even if she barely remembered the passion of either.

"Rumer, what are you saying?"

"I think the kids and I will stay here with Grandma for awhile."

"How long is awhile?"

"I don't know." She didn't. Running around Baltimore, Maryland "playing house" with Luke wasn't going to do anything for her or her children. She wanted the marriage she'd thought she had.

There was a knock at her bedroom door.

"Yes, Grandma." She tried to erase the anger and sadness from her voice.

"Breakfast is ready, honey. I already have the kids at the table. We're waiting on you."

"Okay." She turned her attention back to the phone. "Luke, I really have to go. I'll call you back later."

"Rumer..."

"Yes."

"Rumer, I am not gay."

That's what he wanted to say. No, I love you. No, I miss the kids. No, kiss the kids for me. Only, that he's not gay.

RUMER

How was she supposed to believe that or anything he said? If he wasn't gay, then why all the secrets?

"Luke, I don't know what to think about any of this. I need time to think about things. Time without you. Give me that. Please." The emotions flowing through her were too extreme. She thought she'd say something she didn't mean, or something she did, and never be able to "fix" what was wrong between them. She didn't even know if she should want to fix it. "I'll call you later, okay."

"I will wait for you to call me when you're ready to come back home. I'll be here."

Rumer breathed a sigh of relief as she cleared dishes from the breakfast table. After eating, her grandmother normally disappeared for a short nap, which would give her a little time alone. Lying to her grandmother was hard, but remembering the lies was even harder. There were a few times when she was sure she'd been caught, but her grandma didn't dig, or ask questions. She just smiled and tried to find more ways to coax a giggle or coo from Tyler or a laugh from Maddie.

After settling Ty down for a nap, and ensuring Maddie was content with plenty to occupy her time— coloring books, toys, and puzzles, Rumer relaxed with a cup of coffee onto the couch, which welcomed her like an old familiar friend. But, it wasn't long before soft creaks of the old wood floor alerted her of when her grandmother decided to join her.

"So, sweetheart, when are you going to tell me what's really going on?" The small woman swept a hand along the back of her dustcoat before she sat beside her. Her thin frame barely shifted the cushions of the couch.

She thought about lying again, but her entire being was exhausted. Talking to an empty room could only solve so much. If she discussed it with her friends, then everyone would know. And she wasn't sure just what she knew. So, she decided to tell her the truth. All of it. She watched her grandmother's expression as she shared her story. The older woman had a great poker face. She didn't see anger, but she did see concern fill brown eyes partially concealed by glasses. When Rumer finished, she sat staring into her coffee. The warm liquid had soothed her when she first curled up on the couch, but now it had cooled. She hugged the ceramic mug closer to her chest anyway.

"Sweetheart, I'm sorry this happened to you." Grandma Mae moved closer. "But, Luke is going through a lot right now. He could probably use a friend."

What? "Grandma, what about me? What about how I feel?" *Betrayed by Grandma!*

"Sweetheart," her grandmother reached out and ran a small hand across Rumer's face as she spoke, "I know you're hurting, but he's scared. He's losing his family. He doesn't know how this will affect his career, and his volunteer work both at church and the center. As scary as it is for you, it's scarier for him."

"What about our family? Our marriage?"

"Sweetheart, that's what I'm talking about." Her grandmother shifted her position, and trained her brown bespectacled eyes on her. "What I mean is that for a man like him, this makes him question a lot. If it was another woman, that would be different, but this...this will be difficult for him."

"And what about me and the kids? Are we supposed to hold his hand and help him? Who helps us?" She found herself growing angrier with her grandmother the longer they talked.

"Think about it, sweetie, you have been his best friend for many years. The two of you have your family, and now this happens."

She hadn't thought about that, but true, she didn't exactly see Gabriela fitting into his family, or circle of friends.

"Grandma, I don't know what I'm supposed to do. What do I tell the kids—well, Maddie? Our friends?"

"What you tell Maddie depends on what the two of you do. The rest isn't important. The two of you have to work it out together. You have to talk to him. You can't run."

She snuggled into the couch, and sipped from her cold coffee. Running was easier. "I don't know. I need some time to think."

RUMER

Her grandmother smiled. "Well, take all the time you need. How often do I get to spend time with you and my babies?"

Maddie ran into the room searching for someone to play with.

Grandma Mae cut her off as she bee-lined toward Rumer. "Come on, sweetie, Ganny will color with you."

Rumer watched as Maddie led her grandmother out of the room a little too roughly, but her grandmother didn't complain. She laughed and followed behind her.

Alone. Rumer sat staring out the window into the overgrown brush of the backyard where she'd played as a kid. She'd have to ask Grandma about the lawn service Luke paid for. They were supposed to come out every two weeks. She'd cut it while she was in town until she figured out was what happening.

When she moved to D.C. for college and then Baltimore to follow the love of her life, she'd always thought she'd return, but not like this. Not because she was running from a failed marriage. What her grandmother had said was true. She had been Luke's best friend, and he, hers. That was one of the best parts of their relationship. They could laugh and talk as easily as she could with any of her girlfriends. Her friends had always envied that about their relationship. Now, she'd lose that, and everything she worked for for years.

Resting her head on the side of the couch, she let her eyes scan the familiar room. The walls were filled with photo after photo of her, her mother, her father, her children and Luke, and so many others. She'd created a room similar in her own home. The hallways of her house were lined with family photos. She thought she was capturing her family history. Creating something for her children to one day look back on and share with their own spouses and children.

She watched as tears she'd held back fell into the cold coffee she gripped. Each drop created little ripples that began in the middle of the cup and softened as they spread.

Alone on a couch crying into my coffee. Great. Could I be more pathetic?

Chapter Four

Rumer stood in the dim brightness of the nightlights casting a starry green glow over her sleeping children. Ty normally fought sleep. Stretched out on his back, he slept quietly while Maddie snored in her bed across the hall. Weeks of hiding out at her grandmother's hadn't erased her problems. It had only allowed her to have time to think about what she wanted. And what she wanted was her husband and family. She just no longer thought it was totally possible to have everything. No matter how much Luke swore he hadn't slept with Gabriela or claimed he loved Rumer, her heart wasn't happy.

But, didn't she owe him and her children the opportunity to be a family? To be whole?

Before sunset, she kissed her grandmother on the cheek, and with her car fully loaded, she headed back down the road to Baltimore. What would happen when she arrived? She didn't know, but she couldn't avoid Luke forever.

The familiar squeak of the garage door didn't feel as welcoming as she'd hoped. But, it did succeed in waking her children, and alerting Luke to her arrival. She'd decided not to tell him when she was returning because she changed her mind every day. Only at the insistence of her grandmother and a desire to give her children a "traditional" home was she parking her car beside his instead of filing for divorce.

She didn't know how long she'd sat there gripping the steering wheel, counting the legs of Maddie's dolls poking out of boxes earmarked for donation. The knock on the drivers' side window startled her. She jumped as she turned to look into the brown eyes of the man she'd loved for ten years. The only man she'd ever been intimate with. The father of her children.

She lowered the window, and familiar scents wafted through. How many years had they spent turning the empty house into a home?

"Hi." The simple word stuck in her throat.

His eyes only left hers for a moment as he checked the children in the backseat. "Hi." He paused. "I'm glad you and the children are home." He reached in to touch her shoulder, but she moved, and he pulled away. "I missed all of you." He opened the door, and waited for her to exit.

She turned the car off, and popped the trunk. The dull thud finally woke Maddie.

"Daddy," Maddie squealed.

How could I take that away from either of them?

He rounded the car to where Maddie sat, and reached in to unbuckle her and lifted her from her seat. He hugged her to his chest. "I missed you pumpkin." He kissed her on her cheek.

"Daddy, we had fun with Ganny."

"You'll have to tell me all about it later." He looked over Maddie's shoulder at Rumer. "I'll take her inside and get her ready for bed." He glanced at Ty. "You grab him, and I'll come back for the bags. Okay?"

"Okay." After closing the garage door, she scooped a sleeping Tyler from his car seat and followed behind Luke up the steps into the laundry room.

She put Tyler to bed, and walked to Maddie's room. She paused outside the door and listened. Luke was reading to Maddie from one of her favorite books. Maddie preferred when Luke read her bedtime stories because he did voices for each character. Some nights he'd have to read three or four books because she simply wouldn't fall asleep. Laughter does that. As she begged for one more book, Rumer heard him promise to read more to her tomorrow.

I never should've taken her father away from her. I shouldn't have taken his children from him.

Luke flicked off the light as he walked out of Maddie's room.

"Lub you, Daddy," Maddie yawned.

"Love you, too, sweetie." He stopped when he saw her lurking by the door. "Sorry. Are you on your way in to say goodnight?" he asked.

"No, it's okay." She turned to walk away. Where to? She didn't know. Maybe she'd sleep in the guest room, or the family room.

"Wait." He walked up behind her and grabbed her hand. "Can we talk?"

She turned and allowed her eyes to meet his. "It's late and I'm tired." She pulled away. "Let's talk tomorrow."

"I've given you weeks. Don't you think I deserve answers this time?"

His voice wasn't harsh and his eyes weren't mean, but still she could barely bring herself to look into his sad stare. But, she wasn't sure why. Guilt. Hope. Sadness. Anger. Whatever it was, it scrambled her brain, and made it hard for her to think.

He'd had longer to deal with everything than her. And he expected her to just be okay. She wasn't. Coming back to the house had been hard enough. "Yes, but—"

"No. No more." With her hand held firmly in his, he led her to his office, on the other side of the house, and closed the door behind them.

Luke sat at his computer desk, while Rumer perched in an old office chair across the room, confused about what to do next. He'd rehearsed a million things to say to her, but nothing seemed right. It was obvious from her downturned eyes that the whole topic was equally as uncomfortable for her. How do you tell the mother of your children you've somehow fallen in love with someone else, and that that someone else was born a man? When he discovered Gabriela

35

had kept a secret from him, he'd cut off all communication with her. But, it hadn't stopped the love that had already begun to claim him. He never should've been in a situation that allowed him to fall in love with another woman. Now, it could cost him his family.

"Rumer, I've never been with another woman as long as we've been married," he said with as much conviction as possible. Rumer didn't speak, but she lifted her eyes to meet his. "Gabriela and I have never been together. One night we kissed, and that one night, that one time, is when she told me who she was."

"You didn't know?" she asked.

"No." He considered his words, "We worked together at the center." He stood and walked to the nearby window and stared into the darkness outside. It magnified the dread that filled his mind. He turned away from it, and leaned against the windowsill. "Our conversations turned friendly, over time. We'd meet for coffee, away from the center. And, the more I saw her, the more I wanted to see her."

"You were working at a center for LGBT... didn't you once think she might be different?"

Her use of the word different hit him hard. She thought he was different, too. "Everyone at the center isn't gay. I'm not." He wasn't sure what to think about himself. Maybe he was. His brother had been.

She blinked at his words, but didn't say anything.

"You know I work at the center because my brother committed suicide. Being a young black male and gay in Baltimore wasn't good when we were young." He moved the chair from his desk closer to her and sat. "Many people there are just like me. They volunteer and work at the center because their lives have been affected by hate and people's small minds."

"Are you calling me 'small minded' because I won't accept that my husband has fallen in love with a man?"

She said it to wound him. The words weren't those of the woman he'd loved for ten years, but those of a woman he'd hurt. "Maybe I deserved that because I should've told you. I know I should've stopped it." He reached for her hands, and for a moment the memories of their life together singed their grasp. Then she pulled them away. "I love you, Rumer. I would do anything to save our family. I don't know how to fix this. Please, tell me."

He watched as tears streamed down her cheeks. Everything in him screamed to reach out and gather her up in his arms, but he feared she'd jerk away in disgust. He searched his brain for anything he could do to take away the pain he'd caused her. How could he erase the past weeks, months?

"What do you want me to do?" she asked through hiccupped cries. "Forget my husband loves someone else?"

"I want my family," he said.

"Me, too. But, it would be a lie." She paused. "Who would the lie be for? Me. You. Your job. Our family?"

"We could go to counseling. We could—"

"Counseling. For what? What would I learn that I don't already know? How would I compete with Gabriela?"

"There's no competition. You are my wife. I won't break that commitment. No matter what."

"But, maybe you should. Maybe we both should." She stood. "I'll sleep in the guest room tonight. We'll talk about this more when my headache goes away." She closed her eyes for a second, placed two fingers to her right temple and massaged, slowly.

Luke wanted to stop her. But, what would he say. He'd said everything. He had to find a way to convince her.

I have to fall out of love with Gabriela.

Chapter Five

Luke sat and stared at the windowless walls of his small office located at the center. The office was barely large enough for the small desk and chairs it housed, but they'd made space for him. A small room for him to do his work. The work which had led him to his own destruction. He wanted to blame it on something, someone. But, truthfully, he couldn't. He'd felt a connection with Gabriela the moment he saw her. She hadn't been one of his regular appointees. One day, he'd struck up a conversation with her. Not her with him. She was beautiful. Not that Rumer wasn't. Rumer was his perfect girl next door. The woman who'd given herself to him and only him. The mother of his children. But, Gabriela intrigued him. She carried herself in a way that drew his attention. This couldn't be about sex because he hadn't slept with her.

He maneuvered to reach into his back pocket and retrieve his wallet. He ran his fingers across the warm worn leather. Maddie had given it to him with such pride one Father's Day. The anger building inside of him fought with the love he had for Gabriela. How could he throw away everything he had for a woman he didn't know? Why? He loved his wife and his children.

He opened the wallet and freed the picture of his smiling family from its plastic prison. Rumer was pregnant in the picture. Maddie hugged her mom with such love that the muscles in his chest tightened just from staring at the picture. What if he never had the chance to see that love in his children's eyes again? What if they looked at him the same way Rumer did every time he came near her?

She hates me.

RUMER

There was a knock on the office door. He didn't have any appointments. In fact, no one knew he was there. He didn't want to go home, and the center was the only place he had to go.

Another knock on the door. "Come in," he said.

"Are you busy?" Sebastian, Gabriela's brother and owner of the center, swung the door wide, in his normal way. "Can we talk?"

"What's on your mind?" He placed the family portrait back in its spot, and stuffed the wallet back in his pocket.

"You. And my sister." Sebastian flipped around one of the chairs and straddled it. He rested his folded arms across the back of the chair, and waited.

"What are you talking about?" He didn't know what Gabriela had or hadn't said, but he wasn't offering any details.

The man lifted a bushy eyebrow at him. "I don't know what happened between you and Gabriela, but I wanted to tell you she had her surgery." The man stood and walked toward the door. "She could use a friend."

"I can't..."

"My sister hasn't told me anything about what happened between the two of you, but I know her, and I'm not stupid." He shoved his fisted hands into his pockets. "I know you were important to her, and I know you're married."

"I wasn't trying to hurt her." He forced himself to face the glare of a brother who loved his sister. "I don't know how what happened with your sister happened. But, I love my family."

"I'm not saying you don't love your family. You're the counselor; but, is it okay to lie to yourself, or to them?"

"I'm not lying to anyone." The sound of his own voice told him his words weren't true.

"You should bring your wife here. Let her see what you do, and how you do it."

He would never want to hurt Rumer in that way. Why would he throw her into the middle of everything she feared? "I could never do that to her."

"Why? Because you're afraid of what she'll think? Or, because you're scared to find out the truth about yourself?"

"I know who I am... I know who I am." He repeated the words as if it made them truer.

"We all think we know who we are until something or someone challenges us."

Sebastian closed the door behind him. Who in the hell did this guy think he was? When he first began to volunteer they'd discussed Luke's brother. Sebastian thought he could trust the guy. Maybe he'd be different from the other freaks and gawkers he'd had come through the doors. It's hard to find reliable help. People think they are open-minded until they see a three-hundred pound man dressed in fishnets and wig. Their attitudes change fast.

Luke had been volunteering at the center for months, and he'd had no problem with him until he saw him spending more and more time with his sister. Gabriela had had her heart broken enough times by men like this one. Guys who found themselves attracted to Gabriela because she was beautiful, but whenever she told them the truth about who she was they disappeared as fast as they came.

This one was worse because, as far as he knew, he was the only one that had been married. Gabriela had tried to keep it all a secret from him, but he spent night and day in the center. It was easy to see them coming in early or leaving late. How could he ignore his sister falling in love?

Since they were kids he'd watched Gabriela fight and not back down. High school had been hell. He was older, so there were a lot of times when he wasn't there to back her up. And the school wasn't always on her side either. He lost count of how many schools their parents had transferred her in and out of because she refused to go to school dressed as a boy. They tried counseling and prayed that she'd change. That she'd grow out of it. But, that never happened.

RUMER

It didn't make life any easier for him. By the time he was sixteen, he'd slept with every girl in their neighborhood. He didn't want anyone questioning him. But, it didn't matter because they still asked until he made them moan his name, and cry and into his parents' phone as he broke up with them. Between black-eyes, busted lips, and condoms, he tried to solve all his problems –and Gabriela's, too.

This one he may not be able to solve with his fists, but if the man was foolish enough to bring his wife to the center, he would teach him what it felt like to have your heart toyed with... the hard way.

Luke sat with his head in his hands. Gabriela had had her surgery. She was lying in a hospital somewhere. He was a monster. He had to visit her. What would it say about him, if he didn't?

The vibration of the phone on his hip surprised him.

"Hello."

Rumer's voice was low and unsure. "I hope I'm not disturbing you, but Maddie has a stomach ache. Can you stop on the way to the house and pick up something for her?"

She'd asked the question as if he wouldn't. As if it would be a problem for him to stop and do something for his daughter. "Of course." She didn't ask, but he added. "I'll be home soon. I'm leaving now."

"Oh, okay."

Maybe bringing her to the center to let her see what he does would ease her mind. Maybe it would help him, too. "Rumer, you don't have to answer me now, but I had a talk with Sebastian. He owns the center." She doesn't need to know he's Gabriela's brother. "He thought you might understand more about what I do and more about the center if you came. If you visited or volunteered."

"What? Why?"

"If you come you'll see the center isn't much different from any other place. People need help and we give it. Housing. Jobs. Health. Legal. Whatever they need."

"I don't think—"

"No, don't give me a yes or no. Not now." He was afraid that if she said no there would be no talking her into it. The more he thought about what Sebastian said, the more it made sense. She'd see nothing was wrong with him. He was the same man she married. "We can discuss it more when I get home." He wanted to hang up before she had a chance to respond, but he waited.

"I don't know. I'm not sure..."

"We could get a babysitter. You wouldn't have to commit to many days or anything. Just think about it. I'll be home soon."

He hung up the phone and stood to leave. This was good. This was real good. Rumer was one of the best people he knew. She had a degree in social work. If she saw the center and spent time with the people, she'd understand. She'd forgive him and they'd be able to save their marriage. Their family.

Chapter Six

Rumer sat in her car in the side parking lot staring at the three-story building trying to understand why she'd agreed to meet Luke at the center. What was the purpose? Did she really need to see this place? Luke had always been able to convince her of anything. But, she'd really had no plans to give in on this one. She discussed it with Grandma Mae, and she wouldn't allow Rumer to hang up the phone without her agreeing to meet him halfway.

Instead of sitting and imagining what she'd see when she walked inside, she calmed herself and exited the car. She hit the lock button on the key fob as she walked up to the building.

I guess this is halfway.

She rounded the corner of the building and stopped to take it all in. Simple. If you didn't know what it was, you just wouldn't know. It looked like your typical office building. There was no huge sign or anything, only a small plaque by the front door that identified the center. As she neared the entrance, a group of young men came through the door. Baggy pants, t-shirts, and book bags. If she'd seen them anywhere else, she'd have thought they were the kind of teens that like to skateboard and listen to techno music. Or, college students you see on campuses everywhere.

I guess they could be.

Luke had been held up at work. He'd arranged for Sebastian, the owner, to meet her. Rumer stopped at the security desk, and asked the silver-haired woman for Sebastian. After making a call to announce her, the woman directed her to a small waiting area near the huge front windows.

She watched as some people outside walked by without noticing her while others stared with a hint of curiosity. *Do they know the center's purpose? Do they think I'm here because I need the center?* She switched seats, and sat in the chair furthest from the window.

As she settled into her seat, she heard her name. She glanced up to find a man well over six feet with jet black hair, dark eyes, and familiar features nearing. *How long has he been watching me? Did he see me switch seats?* Shame at her actions gave her greeting a staccato affect.

"H...hello." She stood and extended her hand.

He smiled as he took her hand. "Mrs. Wilson. Nice to finally meet you."

His accent added a twist to the word finally. A twist that for some reason made her wish she'd worn some lipstick or something. She definitely wanted to pull the clip from her hair that held her hair in a "mommy" ponytail, convenient and quick. *What am I thinking? I'm a married woman who is here because my husband wants to save our marriage. And so do I.*

"Thank you." She released his hand. "Luke told me you'd show me around until he arrives."

"It'll be my pleasure."

His accent caressed her. *Pleasure. This man had broken a ton of hearts.*

Sebastian walked behind Rumer because he wanted to be able to assess every inch of her. What made her husband turn his attentions to another woman? From the simple sneakers she wore to the sweat pants and t-shirt, and the clip holding her hair in place she was completely different from his sister. She was exactly the good little church girl he expected Luke to have at home. Gabriela would never walk out of the house without make-up. The stiffness of Rumer's movements told him she was very conscious of him, or maybe she was just uncomfortable in her surroundings. He had no plans to make it any easier on her or Luke. In fact, his plans were exactly the opposite.

"Rumer," he began, "my office is just to the right when you reach the top of the stairs." Sure they could've taken the elevator, but the stairs provided a much nicer view from his position behind her. And it gave him time to check out how she reacted to the sights and sounds of his center. No matter what he had planned, he did need help, and from what Luke told him, she could help him out big time. He couldn't take his eyes off her body. As she climbed the steps holding onto the railing as if she'd fall, he let his eyes roam from the thickness of her thighs to the roundness of her bottom. He knew their youngest was six months old. Gabriela had told him. He didn't know what Rumer's body looked like before the baby, but if he ever saw the kid he'd thank him for his mommy's luscious curves.

He watched as she entered his office and quickly put her back against a wall. It may have hidden her bottom, but it only drew his attention to her small and, yet, full breasts.

"Please..." He positioned a chair for her to sit. "Have a seat."

"Thank you." She crossed her feet at the ankles, and placed her hands in her lap.

His cell phone beeped. "Excuse me." He pulled it from his hip pocket, read the text and then placed the phone on his desk. The text didn't please him. He tempered his anger, and focused on the woman in front of him. "Sorry about that. Luke didn't tell me what exactly you want to learn or do, so maybe you can fill me in." That was true, but he knew why Luke wanted her there, even if Luke wasn't ready to admit it, and she didn't know. It involved his sister, and he'd seen it before. Too many times.

"I'm not sure..." she hesitated, "I...Luke wanted me to become more familiar with the center because it's so important to him."

Important.

"Well, maybe you can tell me what you're interested in."

"I've been a stay-at-home mom for the last three years. I do a lot with the children's program at our church, and I have a degree in social work."

Modest. She had two degrees in social work and a few certifications. When Luke laid out her education and training, he'd been even happier with his plan. The center could use the help for a few months 'til things got back on track. And if he could get it for free or cheap that would help his budget a lot.

She stopped and stared at her hands. "Before we had children, I worked at one of the colleges helping students connect with communities through community service programs."

"If you can convince college kids to volunteer, instead of partying, you're good." He flashed his most reassuring smile.

The soft unguarded laugh that followed his words surprised him. His expression must've given him away because she quieted her laughter too quickly for him. But, the vibration of her shoulders continued and drew his attention to her creamy brown skin. He didn't see a stitch of make-up on her, but her skin glowed. He scanned every inch of it, and the longer he looked, the more his fingers itched to touch her.

"Sebastian," she said, softly.

How many times had she said his name? From her fidgeting, he could tell she'd probably said it more than once. "I'm sorry, I was thinking that maybe you could assist us with our college student program." He paused, not because he needed to think, but because she moved to adjust her position and that simple movement thrust her small breasts forward in a way that made him think this game—his game— would be a lot of fun. "Our program might be a little different. It's not about community service. It's a group program to help them cope with their sexuality."

"I don't know if I would be the right person for a program like that. I don't have the proper training."

"Luke said that you have your Master's in Social Work, like me." He waited. "He also said you have a certification as a school social work specialist. That more than qualifies you to work with groups to manage conflict resolution and crisis intervention."

"I'd need to renew." She said almost to herself.

"That's no problem. We can help you with that." If he was totally honest with her, he'd tell her he had to let go of a few jerks: one who thought the center was his own personal paradise, and the other who wasn't dependable. She cancelled her group more than she held it. "When do you want to begin?"

Before she could answer, Luke walked into the office. Sebastian couldn't determine exactly what the man was thinking as he entered, and he didn't really care. But, he did know where he'd just come from. According to Gabriela's text. He returned his attention to Rumer. He wanted her to say yes. He'd promise her almost anything.

"I'm sorry I'm late. I had to take care of a few things at the office."

Liar!

Luke leaned down and kissed the top of Rumer's head.

Sebastian watched. Once they'd loved each other, he knew it; but, now they pretended. Why?

Luke pulled up a chair beside Rumer's. "Did you have guys have time to walk the center and talk about volunteering?" he asked his question of both of them.

"We've been talking, but we didn't tour." Sebastian responded. "I can walk with you, or you can give her a personal tour." He paused and directed his attention to Rumer. "But, she still hasn't told me if she's interested in working with the group. We could really use the help with Paul and Bianca gone."

"Rumer, if you want to do it, we could put the kids in daycare, or ask my parents to help. Maybe Grandma Mae would come down and help out for a little while," Luke said.

Sebastian relaxed a little. Luke was going to do the negotiating for him.

"I didn't think you'd want me to be so involved. I thought maybe a few times a month or something." She adjusted herself in her chair. "Do you need a response today, or can I think about it for a few days?"

Sebastian couldn't miss Luke's reaction. His shoulders dropped a little before he took a deep breath and spoke. "No rush, right Sebastian?" He kissed her on the cheek. "Take all the time you need."

Sebastian knew exactly why the creep wanted her to work at the center so badly; he didn't care about that. But, he'd help him because he had his own reasons. "No, no rush. But, the kids could use someone like you, Rumer. The center could use the help. Our budget is stretched. We could give you a stipend like we did the others based on how many hours you put in, but we'd love the help." He smiled in a way that he knew women loved. A way he'd practiced since he had to smile for both him and his brother.

"Okay, I'll think about it," she responded. "Thank you."

"Thanks, Sebastian," Luke said. Holding Rumer's hand, he stood, pulling her to her feet as he rose from his chair. "Come on, I'll show you around the center before we head home."

Sebastian watched them leave his office. Their tense posture told him everything. He didn't know what Rumer did or didn't know, but he thought this might be easier than he'd planned. Because one thing was painfully obvious— Luke had broken her heart. He didn't want to hurt her because she was an innocent in this; but, Luke, on the other hand, deserved everything he got, including being alone.

Chapter Seven

Luke tightened his grip on Rumer's small hand as he guided her through the halls of the center. Maybe this was a stupid idea. Maybe this would do the exact opposite of what he wanted. But, it was too late, now. He'd talked her into coming, and now he had to figure out what to do next. He saw the way Sebastian looked at her. And the man had a reputation. He'd never heard of him crossing the lines at the center. But from the number of women showing up asking about him and the gossip he tried to ignore, he knew the guy had more than his share of one night stands.

As he glanced at his wife beside him, he knew exactly what the man saw. A beautiful woman. A woman who had once captured his attention from across the campus. He still remembered the way she smiled and the laughter that once he thought he'd never tire of hearing. He hadn't seen or heard either, lately, and he was the reason. She'd returned home to him and she was with him now, but a knot twisting in his gut told him nothing was permanent.

What will my kids think of me? They are young now, but they'll eventually understand. My family? My friends? My job? The church?

Rumer could change his life, if she didn't forgive him.

He didn't know if she'd eaten or not, but the last stop on their tour was the cafeteria. He thought it would be a great place for her to see a cross-section of the people that come through the doors of the center. They walked through the lines making their selections. The knots in his stomach had stolen his appetite. But, he watched as she filled her tray with salad, soup, and bread. He chose a table tucked away in a corner. Not to hide, but to talk.

He focused on the tray of food because he didn't know where to begin. She had barely spoken during the tour. He'd thought she'd ask questions, and maybe he'd be able to get a feel for what she was thinking, but it didn't happen. The only time he saw her react was when they passed by a group of men practicing a song in one of the meeting rooms. As their voices harmonized the sad lyrics, she stopped and leaned against the wall as if the words spoke to her.

Although she had a tray of food, she only nibbled on the bread. Holding the roll in her hand, she broke small pieces off and ate one after the other. Her eyes didn't seem to focus on anything. She just stared at nothing.

"I'm sorry." He didn't know what else to say. "I don't know what I was thinking." He could feel the acid in his stomach crawling up his throat. "I thought bringing you here would show you that this center is like any other outreach program anywhere. That it's no different, but I guess it is. It is different in many ways, but we still do things to help people. I'm making a difference." He paused. "But, if you don't want to be involved... if you want me to stop... I understand."

Moments passed with her saying nothing. She stared into her plate of food, and just as he was about to give up hope that she'd ever speak to him again, she said, "I'm sorry, too."

He reached for one of her hands resting on top of the table. "Why?"

"I don't know what I expected. I'm not really sure why I came." Her eyes scanned the room. "But, I think I like it."

"You do?" He was surprised.

"I researched it last night before I came. So many people in the community said great things. People who've used the center had even better testimonials. And Sebastian, according to the website, did all of this because of his own childhood and his brother. Like you." She used her free hand to drink from her glass of water. "I've been out of the 'real' world for so long it's crazy. I'd love to build a program to work with college students. I just don't know if I can build a strong enough program."

He was so happy he thought his heart would explode. "I am confident in you. And I could help." He gently squeezed her hand.

Sweetly and sadly, she smiled. It wasn't the smile that captured his heart from across the college campus, but maybe with time, he'd see that one again.

Rumer propped more pillows behind her back to cushion her from the wooden bars of the bed's headboard. The guest room's queen sized bed slept well enough, but since she'd returned to their home in Baltimore, she didn't sleep. If she was lucky, she'd get four or five hours a night and with two young children, one barely out of diapers, that was hard. She hadn't been much fun for anyone to be around. Good thing Tyler was too young to understand, but Maddie, Rumer believed, understood everything.

She reached across the bed to grab the remote she tossed there earlier, and clicked the power button. The TV popped to life, and she hit the mute button. She didn't want to wake the kids. Besides she didn't care what was on the thing anyway, she just wanted to think about something other than the center, Luke, Gabriela and...Sebastian. She'd replayed every word both men had said to her over and over again in her head. But, Sebastian, his words... they didn't affect her like Luke's. A mixture of anger, regret, and loss flowed through her when she thought about Luke.

When she let her mind wander to thoughts of Sebastian it was different. And each time, the words had the same affect, even now. She rubbed the tips of her fingers across her goose-bumped skin. Sebastian Ortiz loved women, she knew it. He might love men, too, she didn't know. She'd read the articles, but maybe there was more to him, just like there was more to Luke and his reasons for wanting her to volunteer at the center.

She shut off the TV because it wasn't helping her insomnia. She picked up one of the books she had stacked on the table beside the bed, and flipped it open to the page with the top corner folded. One of her favorite romance novelists. She may not have the fairy tale in her real life, but nobody said she couldn't feed her mind with the beautiful words of a book.

As she turned the pages, she envied the heroine and desired the hero. Geez, she flung the book across the room. *Why? Why can't life be more like books? Okay, so maybe I don't want vampires sucking on my neck, or werewolves chasing me through the woods. But, what about the loyalty and commitment written about on those pages? You don't' read stories about a woman dedicating ten years of her life to a man only to have him fall out of love with her after she has their second child. After she's fat and dumpy with crap hair and bad skin.*

She flipped over and pushed her face into the pillows to muffle the sound of her sobs. She thought she had her fairy tale, but they just don't exist.

Not for me.

Chapter Eight

Sebastian sat next to his sister's recovery bed. They'd recommended that she have full-time care for two weeks. And no matter how much she wanted to leave, he wasn't having it. Their parents couldn't take care of her. He imagined his mother or father helping her with her baths or medications. It would never work. And he couldn't do it either. Not because he wouldn't, but because he had to worry about the center. He checked his watch. He'd have to leave soon because he had a meeting with Rumer and Luke to discuss what her new program would look like.

He stood and wiped wet waves of her dark hair away from her damp forehead. He walked across the room and opened the blinds blocking the sunlight. She loved the sun. Since they were kids she'd always preferred to be outside instead of locked away anywhere. She opened her eyes and stared at him as he neared.

Her eyes tried to focus, but her post-surgical pain had increased. She needed sleep and probably more or stronger meds; he'd check on her in the morning. She hadn't contracted any infections. She was lucky, he'd read a lot about the surgery and too often people got infections near the wound, and had to be treated with even stronger drugs. But, his sister had always been a fighter, and she was healthy. That's all he could ask for. He needed her to be okay.

She tried to move and adjust her position in bed, but from the way she stopped and squeezed her eyes shut he knew that was a bad idea. After a few moments, she opened her eyes and gave him a weak smile. He leaned over the bed, and kissed her on the forehead.

"Mi hermana, don't try to move. They want you to keep everything to a minimum for a little while." He stood and stared into her dark sad eyes. How many times had he seen that same expression? "I'm not sure if he'll be able to come and visit you again." He paused. He wasn't sure if he should tell her the next part. "His wife will be working at the center."

He watched as understanding crossed her face. "Seb...astian, she's a nice woman." Her voice was the old familiar voice from their childhood. He hadn't heard it in so long.

She was worried about Rumer. Her boyfriend's wife. She'd always had a gentle heart. That's why he had to be the one to take care of both of them. That's what he was going to do again. He would take care of Luke and his cheating heart, and maybe have a little fun along the way. Rumer was a nice woman—a beautiful caramel skinned woman—maybe as gentle as his own sister, and he wouldn't try to hurt her. But, Luke deserved everything coming to him.

He smiled as he picked up a cloth from the bedside table and dabbed at sweat on his sister's forehead. "Don't worry little sister. I like her. It's her husband I have a problem with." He knew she wouldn't like those words, but they were the truth. He kissed her cheek.

"It's not his fault." She closed her eyes and swallowed. "Mine." She opened her eyes and reached up to rub the back of her hand along his cheek. "He didn't know until I told him." An odd expression crossed her face. Regret. Sadness. He wasn't sure.

The bastard didn't know, but he still was a married man playing with the heart of the pretty Puerto Rican chick. Did he think his job and money allowed him to do whatever he wanted? Might sound hypocritical, but it wasn't. Sebastian never took a woman to his bed that didn't want it. He always told them where things stood. He liked having different lovers, and he really had no plans of changing that any time soon.

"It's okay. He's a married man. Why was he going out with you?"

She let her arm softly fall back to the bed and rest beside her body. "I knew what I was getting into. He tried to walk away, but I didn't let him."

She was trying to take all the blame on herself, and he wouldn't allow it. He stood and took a few steps back and scanned her weakened body. His sister was only slightly shorter than him, but she'd always had a smaller frame than his. And he consciously made his bigger by working out with weights and playing sports. High school was hell and sports and weights made everyone think twice about what they said to him and his sister. But, no one should ever take her for granted. She could outrun anything, and she worked out in her own way. It all lead to a body that was lean and muscular. It might have been hard for Luke to understand she wasn't a "typical" woman, but he never should've played games with her in the first place. How hard is it to walk away from a woman? Sebastian did it every day.

He began to walk toward the door. "Mi hermana, he could've kept saying no until you got the message."

"Sebastian," she pleaded.

"No." He didn't want to hear any more. He had to get to the meeting. He paused at the door with his hand wrapped around the doorknob. "I'm not going to do anything to the damn idiot." That was true. He planned to do everything to Rumer, and let her do it to him.

Gabriela squinted at him as if she was trying to see inside of his head. See inside of his lie. But, unless she had some super power he didn't know about that wasn't going to happen.

"Te amo," he said as he closed the door behind him.

Chapter Nine

Sebastian walked into the tiny conference room where Luke and Rumer waited and sat in a chair beside Rumer. There were other chairs, but why not make it convenient for her. This way she could easily share the report she wanted to show him.

"Sorry I'm late," he said, mainly for her, but he acknowledged both of them. "I had an appointment that ran a little long."

"No problem." She smiled the sweetest smile.

He let his eyes scan the room. He made a mental note to have painters come and touch up the paint on the walls. He kept searching. There wasn't anything on any of the tables, but there was definitely something soft with a delicious hint of cucumber. Rumer reached over and touched his arm. He stared at the place where her small fingers rested on his bicep. Her hand would never wrap around. She pulled it away, but he could still feel it. There it was again. That scent. Cucumber. It was her.

"Sebastian, are you okay?" she asked.

He looked up to see soft lines of concern etched in her forehead. Even Luke sat staring at him.

"Sorry, yes, I'm fine." What had they been discussing when he got distracted? "Did I miss anything?"

"No, we just arrived," she said. "And Luke has to go to a meeting, so he can't stay long. It'll just be the two of us." A look of uncertainty crossed her face.

He leaned forward to catch Luke's eye. "No worries Luke. I'll take care of her. Just like I know you'd take care of my sister." He smiled as he allowed the words to sink in for Luke.

RUMER

Rumer sat between the two of them, but she was facing Sebastian. She couldn't see the fear in Luke's eyes.

"Sebastian, you have a sister?" she asked.

"Yes," he responded.

"Oh, I thought you had a brother." Her head swiveled between the two men.

"Yes." He knew the answer might confuse her, but he wasn't ready for her to know everything yet. "My brother—"

"Babe, I don't have a lot of time. Can we discuss the program?" Luke asked.

Sebastian could barely control the emotions inside of him. He felt too many at once. But, one thing was certain, Luke hadn't told Rumer that Gabriela was his sister. The bastard was probably leaving the meeting to go and blow more smoke up Gabby's butt. How could he have been so wrong about the dude?

"Sure, sorry." She seemed slightly embarrassed.

"It's okay, I'll gladly tell you everything you want to know when we have the time," he said.

He watched as Luke's posture stiffened. The man understood exactly what he meant. He wouldn't give him forever to tell his wife the whole truth. But, while he waited, he'd take the opportunity to get to know everything he could about Rumer Wilson.

Rumer sat between the two men unsure of what was being unsaid, but she knew Luke too well. Maybe Sebastian had decided he didn't want her help after all. Dread crept through her body. Somewhere between learning of the center's existence, her walkthrough with Luke, and her conversations with her grandmother, she'd decided this would be a great way to use her degree and do something where she could create her own an impact. Not just as Luke's wife.

Insomnia had proved helpful for once. She worked through the night on her idea, and this morning she emailed it to Luke, while he was at work, to review. They both thought it was pretty solid, but if Sebastian hated it, then there was nothing more to be said.

Luke reached over and squeezed her hand. The gentle touch of his hand made her focus, but when she did it was Sebastian's bright white smile and brown eyes that greeted her. His smile widened, and her body responded. Heat flowed through her from the hairs pulled back into her ponytail to the tips of her toes. She didn't know how to handle her body's reaction to a simple smile from this man.

Again she focused on the papers spread on the conference table in front of her. The words and images jumbled together. How could this be happening? She was married. Who cared if it was a lie, and her husband loved someone else. They'd made the decision to try. And trying is what counted, right?

She forced herself to push her confusion aside, and make sense of the pages in front of her. "Sebastian, I'm not sure if what I've designed is what you had in mind, but here goes." She took a deep breath. "I know the center offers all types of programs for members of the LGBTQ community, but because this program is directed at college students, I wanted to have part of my program deal with issues of sex. I know you are aware, but nearly two-thirds of all diagnosed HIV infections are from male-to-male sexual contact. And HIV infections are disproportionately high among African-American and Latino males." She took another deep breath and used the opportunity to take a quick peek at Sebastian. He didn't say anything.

So, she continued. "I met my husband in college, and if my memory serves me right, it's a time when people take advantage of being away from their parents' prying eyes." She thought back to the days of long nights and late mornings. When she and Luke met, they'd grab a blanket, throw it on the ground in their own secret little spot and wouldn't move from that spot until campus security caught them. "Also, I'd like to bring in speakers and discuss abuse and violence. The presentation will give you more information. When you have time to review it, you'll see I have segments that would cover concerns in the workplace and family, too."

Neither man said anything. Maybe she needed to go into more detail. As they flipped through her presentation, she thought maybe she should go and find a drink of water somewhere. The waiting was killing her. Her anxiety mixed with the tension between the two men made the small room even smaller. She wished there was a window to open.

Sebastian finally spoke. "This is great work, Rumer. How long did it take for you to put this together?" He didn't wait for a response. "Because we have connections with clinics in the area, your program to discuss health concerns is perfect. We also have companies that do regular job fairs here, so that dovetails right into your idea about workplace concerns. And the section on abuse and violence we can design with our partnership with the gay and lesbian division of the police department."

Luke wrapped his arm around her shoulder and kissed her on the cheek. "I told you he'd love your ideas."

She was so excited. There was a lot of work to do. After she and Sebastian went over the fine details, she'd have to lock down all the partners and get a schedule set-up. And then they'd be set.

"Are you sure, Sebastian?" she asked because she didn't want to get her hopes up for nothing.

"Positive. Why don't we find something to eat and go over a few more of the details?"

"I wish I could join you two, but I have a meeting I can't miss," Luke said.

"Are you sure, Luke?" she asked. She could feel tension knotting up the chords of her back. She didn't want to do it alone. "No way you can get out of it?"

Luke looked past her at Sebastian. If there was such a thing as telepathy, she'd swear the two men were talking to each other. They definitely had their secrets.

"This will give you a chance to go over the fine details with Sebastian, and then you and I can talk about it later when I get home." He kissed her on the cheek and stood to leave. He stopped and rested a hand on Sebastian's shoulder. "Sebastian, go easy on her. Okay?"

"Man, you have my word. I will take care of her." He smiled.

Luke closed the door behind him, and she was alone.

Alone with Sebastian.

Chapter Ten

Sebastian had managed to coax Rumer into leaving the center and having an early dinner at one of the nearby bistros. She'd had no preference, but the little Greek place he chose was perfect. The cafeteria had too many eyes, and he needed some place a little less public. The woman sitting across from him had surprised him. He hadn't expected the presentation to really be any good. He would've said yes, regardless, and told her what he needed. If she still didn't get it, he'd hold her hand and walk her through it step by step. He had done exactly that for the two people he'd fired. But Rumer—she didn't need anything from him, or Luke.

He watched as she fussed with her silverware and water glass. Then she placed her napkin across her lap. From the movement of her arms, she must've smoothed it to removed wrinkles. When she finally looked up, she caught him staring. He didn't care.

"Sebastian," she said as she tugged at the neckline of the orange blouse resting against her smooth skin.

His eyes followed the soft cottony fabric as it flowed over her small perky breasts down her stomach 'til it disappeared where it met the table. Sebastian didn't know what it was, but from the moment he'd walked into the meeting room, she'd captured his attention. Even now, in the dim light of the restaurant, her skin glowed. Healthy. Smooth. Creamy caramel. Everything in him wanted to reach out and run his fingers down one of her arms to see if her skin felt as smooth and soft as it looked.

"Sebastian," she said again. "Why are you staring at me?"

"Sorry, it's just...you surprised me." Might as well be honest. At least partially. "I didn't expect you to do your homework and be so prepared." Or, to be so beautiful.

She smiled. "Then why did you ask me to volunteer?"

Smart woman. Good question. "Luke knew I needed some help and he knows the budget is tight." That was the truth. "When he said he knew someone, I didn't expect it to be his wife. I didn't want to say no to someone who has worked with us for so long."

She smoothed her hidden napkin again. "So, you would've said yes no matter what?"

"Yes, but he told me you had the credentials. I just wasn't sure" He didn't want her to think...think what...that she wasn't intelligent and beautiful.

"So, not just a favor for Luke."

"No. I have to make sure that I'm providing a service to the people who walk through the doors of the center."

"That makes sense," she said.

The salad she'd ordered, and his gyro finally arrived. He fisted his gyro and raised it to his mouth. He noticed her eyes. They were locked on his hands. He realized he enjoyed her eyes on him, even if they were only staring at his hands.

"Would you like a bite?"

She thrust her fork into her salad and loaded it up. "No, this is just fine."

Again, he let his eyes roam. Her breasts weren't large, but definitely a good handful. And he loved her rear. He'd had a few dreams about it since the first day he met her. She was filled out in all the right places. But, she'd just had a baby, maybe she didn't agree.

"Are you on some kind of diet?"

"No. Not exactly." She focused on slicing a cucumber into smaller pieces.

He didn't know how he knew, but he knew she was lying.

"Not exactly, huh?"

"Well, I did just have a baby six months ago." She smiled, weakly.

He cut off a piece of his gyro and put it on a saucer near her. "You know you want it." He took a bite. "You shouldn't be so concerned about the way you look. You're beautiful." He placed his gyro on his plate and focused on her. This time, when he let his eyes roam, he let her see it. "I'd like to see you without that ponytail," he said and waited for her response. Her only response was to reach up and touch the band holding the ponytail in place. "But, I've seen a lot of moms walking around with those. I guess it's easy."

She ran her hand along her sleek hair 'til it reached the tip of her ponytail. "I don't have much time for myself."

"What will you guys do when you start working at the center?"

"My grandmother will move in with us for a little while. That will be great." She bit into a tomato. "Our kids love her and we don't see her often enough."

"My grandparents are in Puerto Rico. My parents are here, but we don't see them often." That was on purpose. His parents still had a hard time with Gabriela, and they didn't understand why he opened a center for "them."

"You don't get to see them often. Why?" She waited.

"Some families are just complicated."

"I'm sorry," she said. "I don't get to see my father much. He's lives in California."

"Do your kids get to see him?"

"No, he's never seen either of them." Her words were soft and sad.

She continued to surprise him. She was much stronger than she realized. Her husband was a bastard, and so was her father, but she still held her head up and was willing to give something back. He liked her more. "It's his loss. Your kids are lucky to have you."

"Family is important. My grandmother always told me that."

"She's right." He wanted to lift her spirits. "So, tell me more about your plan to help me with the center."

The shadows that had begun to take over the features of her beautiful face began to disappear. She smiled at him, and damn if that didn't make him happy.

Luke didn't know what to do. He sat in the chair beside Gabriela's bed unable to do much more than take in everything. Her dark wavy hair had lost a little of its shine and she, for once, didn't have on make-up, but she was still the same person. He couldn't bear to think of what she'd been through to become the person that rested on the bed beside him.

"Are you just going to sit there?" she asked.

He hadn't realized she'd awakened. "I'm sorry. I didn't want to wake you."

"Is that the only reason?" Her gaze fell to the thin blanket covering her before she captured his eyes again.

He wasn't sure. "Gabby, I...what do you want me to do? This is all—"

"—why did you come here?" Tears fell with the strangled words.

"Because I couldn't let you be here and not come to see you." That was the truth. He'd tried. He wanted to ask Sebastian, but he knew that was a bad idea. The guy already looked at him like he wanted to stick a knife in his heart.

"Does your wife know you're here?"

"No, but she wouldn't object to me seeing a friend in a hospital," he lied.

Gabby's eyes widened. "Even me?"

He ignored the question. "Gabby, what do you want from me?" He paused. "I told you I was married. I told you. And then after...after...what does all of this make me?" He really didn't know. "A liar. A cheater." *Gay.*

"Are those your only concerns?" She swallowed. "Not the fact that I was also born a man?"

He didn't like the raspy sound of her voice. He looked around for something for her to drink. Grabbing a pitcher and a plastic cup, he poured her a tepid cup of water and stood beside her to help her sip. Then, he sat, and tried to think. "Why didn't you tell me?" He'd felt a little betrayed by the omission. He had no right to, because he was married, but he did.

"I didn't mean for anything to happen." She coughed as she repositioned herself in the bed. "I enjoyed our conversations. I loved being near you." She pulled her fingers through the waves of her hair. "You allowed me to get away from so much of the crap I see every day." Tear-filled eyes locked on his. "I loved the way you looked at me."

Her words broke his heart. Not just because of her sadness, but because he'd heard them before. Rumer had said something very similar when he begged her to come back to him. And he'd promised her he'd never looked at a woman the way he had her. That he'd never loved another woman the way he had her. But, as he looked at the woman in front of him, he knew that was only half true. He didn't love them the same, that was true. But, he loved this woman, and he didn't know how to break the bond that had him reaching for her hand. The warmth of it in his hand reminded him of her touch, her kiss. Warm and tender. She had a big heart, like Rumer. But, the two were as different as night and day.

How could he ever justify breaking either of their hearts. He thought he knew what his future held. Children. Grandchildren. Simple life. This woman complicated it all for him, in ways he'd never imagined.

Did he want his old life to be his future? Or, did he allow his heart to take him down a path that was so different?

Chapter Eleven

It took weeks to get all the kinks worked out, but finally they'd received confirmations from all the guest lecturers. The meeting room was painted a bright yellow—no sadness allowed, not even on the walls. And as of last count, they had eight students signed up for Rumer's group. They'd set the limit for ten. So, eight was absolutely freaking great. Luke had offered to assist Rumer on her first day with the students, but she'd refused. Not because she didn't want him there, but because she'd depended on Luke for too long for too much. But, for the life of her, she didn't know why. She loved him, that was true, but her plans had never been get two degrees, get married, have two kids, and done. But, truthfully, she couldn't remember what the plan had been. Get two degrees and take over the world. Ha!

Designing the program along with Sebastian had reminded her of why she loved social work. Why she'd wanted a huge family of her own, but after each promotion Luke received, it seemed they spent less and less time together. It's not that they were unhappy. They took family trips two or three times a year. They had a nice home and a solid bank account, including their retirement plan. And their sex life was adequate, but what was her contribution.

When her father left and started his new family, she found out the hard way how easy it was for some people to forget. Volunteering with different mentor programs, while in college, she discovered that other children weren't as lucky as her. Everyone didn't have a fabulous grandmother who wouldn't let them pull the covers over their head and feel sorry for themselves. She'd attended too many high school graduations that didn't have one parent present. She'd seen too many children drop out of school and not return.

This program, this center could be the opportunity for her to once again find a way to be more than "just" the wife of Luke Wilson.

RUMER

I loved being his wife for ten years. Did he love being my husband?

The small room she and Sebastian chose was perfect. It was on the third level, and had several big windows. It would allow the kids to look out on the city. She knew from some of the late nights she'd spent with Sebastian that the room would have beautiful night views. You could see for miles. Baltimore, situated on the Patapsco River, had a harbor that would rival Old Town Alexandria, Virginia and Annapolis, Maryland, and she was sure many others. Restaurants, the aquarium, the zoo, and other attractions normally had the area teaming with visitors during the day, especially in the summer time. But, most of them didn't hang around for the concerts at night. Maybe because of fear of safety, or maybe they didn't know about them, but either way they were missing out. If the kids attended some of the evening programs she and Sebastian had planned, they'd love it.

She focused her attention back to the chairs in the center of the room. A circle. Inclusion. As she decided to go grab a cup of coffee and turn up the air, she heard her name.

"Mrs. Wilson," the voice said.

She turned to see a petite blond. The innocent face should've been less worried, not so exhausted. The pensive look was like a gut punch. She hoped that she'd be able to help. Maybe her first impression was wrong, and he hadn't been through hell. But, maybe she was right. The pierced eyebrow and baggy pants told her this young man would stand out wherever he went. No matter how tired his expression, his back was straight, and his voice firm. He'd never back down. She knew it. It worried her, but she liked him. He was not afraid.

"Hi," she began, "call me Ms. Rumer."

He smiled. "Kevin."

She made it her goal to see Kevin smile more. When he smiled he made you want to smile, too. A weird nervous excitement made her stomach flutter. Kevin was her first student and, she peeked over his shoulder, there would be seven more. She didn't know what she would or wouldn't be able to do, but she was ready to give it her best shot.

Pain lanced through Gabriela Santiago Perez's entire body as she slowed her walking pace. It'd been almost a month, and maybe she was a little ambitious, but she'd thought she could make it to the end of her parents' block and back without her head exploding from pain. She was wrong. She paused at the mailbox, and looked down the long driveway. She was thankful for the gust of wind that swirled around her. And even more thankful she'd decided to wear a skirt and loose fitting blouse. She stood perfectly still as the warm breeze kissed every part of her skin it could find.

Again, she took another angry measure of the driveway in front of her. God, it was far. She took a second and third deep breath, braced herself, and put one foot in front of the other. Next time, she'd listen to the doctor, and only walk to the end of the driveway and back a few times. But, she felt good after reaching the end of the driveway, and thought she could do more. After all, they were doctors, what did they know about her body. Everything!

There was no way for her to fight the anxiety growing inside of her. She didn't know how her brother had done it, but he'd figured out some way to convince her step-dad, his father, and their mother to care for her in their home. It wasn't that her parents didn't' love her, but her step-dad definitely preferred everyone knew she wasn't his natural child. How many times had she been referred to as Eva's daughter? She'd lost count. Sometimes, she was positive that if her step-dad could erase her from the family, he would.

As soon as she was able to leave, she did. She found a college on the other side of the continent and left. But, her brother had asked her to come back home. And when he told her about his project, she couldn't refuse. She'd never turn her back on him. He was the only person that stood up for her. It hurt her a little every time she thought about how much she felt like she'd stolen from him. He'd never admit to it, but she knew because of how cruel people were to her all her life, her brother had practically cut himself off from loving anyone. He took much more pleasure out of making people love him, and then taking his love away. Maybe she did the wrong thing by coming back. She never wanted to open up old wounds for her brother. But, she missed him, terribly.

The day she'd arrived, he'd picked her up from the airport, and it was like no time had passed. He picked her up in a huge bear hug and only put her down after she complained about going unconscious from lack of oxygen.

With her out for months and his firing two other people he would be short handed. He needed her, and she was laid up like a helpless baby. She tried to quietly open the door, but the squeaking screen door needed oil or something. Her step-dad's head popped around the corner. His eyes didn't move off her until she reached the door of her room—a converted family room on the first level. There was no way she'd be able to climb steps to her childhood room. When she turned to shut the door, her step-dad had disappeared.

She sat on the bed, kicked off her flip-flops, and repositioned herself to lie down. Nothing ever felt so good. She exhaled, long and deep, when her head hit the mattress. She closed her eyes and began to drift off to sleep. Images of Luke wouldn't allow her to rest. She'd hurt him and his family. He was right; he'd stopped their conversations, and made everything clear. She wouldn't let it go. If some crazy chick walked up on her she wouldn't have handled it like Rumer. Attack first, and then ask questions was her motto. She'd found out the hard way that asking questions first can get you a busted nose and black eye. She smiled at that because she knew her brother would love a woman like Rumer with her spunk. Gabriela owed Luke and Rumer an apology. She had no right to expect him to leave his family for her. He'd never meant to be unfaithful or deceitful in any way. Isn't that what attracted her to him in the first place? His decency. His loyalty to family? Even after she told him, he didn't recoil from her in disgust. Instead, he was honest. And scared. He didn't know what it meant for him. For his family. For his children

She squeezed her eyes tighter and fisted her hands into the sheets trapped underneath her. How had she become so cruel a person? Why had she destroyed a happy family? She willed herself to get well because she needed to get up out of bed to help her brother, apologize to Luke, and find Rumer Wilson to apologize. If the woman clawed her eyes out, she deserved it.

Chapter Twelve

Sebastian Ortiz Perez hit the send button on the text to Rumer, and leaned back into the hard unyielding plastic chair that served as his desk chair. It was easy to have a conversation with her no matter how it was done. Text. Call. Face-to-face, his preference. He loved being able to watch her light up as she discussed what the kids were doing at school, in the group, and how the meetings were helping them in small every day ways. The group's success was important to the center, and he needed to be updated regularly if any of the kids were having problems she couldn't handle.

It's not because she's beautiful and has a body that makes me curious how she's the mother of two children.

Everything he was doing was for his sister. Luke needed to learn what it felt like to have someone you loved hurt you. Trouble was, the more time he spent with Rumer, the more confused his situation became. If he could get her into his bed that would be great; it would clear everything up, instantly. But, there was no escaping the pain in her eyes when she talked about Luke. She might not love him the way she once did, but she definitely cared for him, and she wasn't going to allow anyone to hurt him. It was obvious in the fact that she hadn't divorced him. Instead, they were working on it. What was there to work on? He needed them divorced.

The sooner the better!

Luke was the worst kind of man, one who took advantage of another more vulnerable person.

He shifted in his seat, and let his gaze focus on the lights he knew to be coming from the Baltimore Harbor. It was too far away for clear details, but he could see the water and the lights. The meeting room Rumer used had a better view, and that's one of the reasons he wanted her to use it. He'd cleared out most of his stuff before he showed it to her. She'd never remember that it was his office before. She hadn't worked in the building long enough. And he'd told everyone else he thought her program would eventually expand and she would need the slightly larger room.

He scanned the beige walls of his office, and thought maybe he should do like Rumer and brighten the place up. Maybe it would chase away a few of the shadows in his heart. A knock on his open office door caught his attention.

Luke!

The idiot walked into his office as if he'd invited him. He reached out to his phone resting on his desk beside his computer and held it in his hand. The warmth of the phone grounded him. "What do you need?" he asked, but not in a nice way.

The man pulled up a seat. "Why are you spending so much time with Rumer?" He locked his gaze on Sebastian. "I've never seen you do that with anyone else."

He wanted to smile and say, you know why, but he said, "I didn't expect her to be so good. I think she can help me train other staff, and we could use her program's model, too."

"She's always been an intelligent woman." He let his hand slide over his bald head before he brought it back to his lap. "I don't deserve her."

"No, you don't." Nothing wrong with agreeing with the man.

Luke searched Sebastian's face as if he had a question. "She and I are not divorcing."

That wasn't a question. Sebastian waited.

"I don't want you to tell her about Gabriela. I will tell her."

"You played your game with my sister." He squeezed the phone, and reeled in his anger. "I don't appreciate it. I didn't think you were that type of man," he said because he didn't.

"I never meant to hurt her, Rumer, or anyone." He paused. "We would talk after my last counseling session, and that led to dinners, and that led to this mess." With the last words, Luke flipped his hands over showing his palms. He stared at them as if he could see the mess in his hands.

"Luke, you are a married man. Why would you disrespect your marriage by going out with another woman?" A woman like Rumer deserved a different kind of man. A man that wouldn't lie to her about why he came home late, or find a reason to sneak out early.

"I thought of Gabriela as a friend. I didn't realize what was happening until it hit me. Until we kissed."

Sebastian's back stiffened a little at thinking about his sister's hope when she kissed him. "You knew who she was."

"I knew she was your sister, but I didn't know everything."

Gabriela had told Sebastian that, but still the man broke her heart. "What does it matter? You led her on. You had no right." Sebastian could barely hold onto his anger.

Luke threw his hands up, palms toward Sebastian. The universal sign for stop. "No, I didn't lead her on. I never took my ring off. I never kept anything from her. And when I told her I couldn't go further, she found Rumer and told her." Anger colored Luke's expression at his last thought.

Gabriela may have told her part of it, but she didn't tell her everything. "When will you tell Rumer?" That would make it a lot easier for him to swoop in and be her hero.

"I haven't seen Gabriela since she moved in with your parents. And she won't respond to my calls or text messages."

"So," Sebastian said.

"I don't know when or if she's coming back to the center."

"Oh, so, if she doesn't come back, you'll never tell Rumer?" In that case he'd have to tell her himself. How could he tell her without her thinking he was keeping secrets from her, too? He didn't like that thought at all. He released his phone before he crushed it. "I won't keep my sister away. I brought her back here to help me with this place. And I feel like you took advantage of her."

"Sebastian, I'm asking that you allow me to tell my wife the whole truth, myself." He stood to leave. "We don't need your interference in our marriage."

Sebastian smiled as he watched Luke walk out the door. The man knew exactly what Sebastian had in mind, and that would just make it more fun.

Luke stopped by Rumer's group before he left, maybe she'd be ready to go. But, he knew that was a pretty foolish thought. He stood at the door of the bright yellow room, and his anger at Sebastian spiked again. The guy had given up his office for Rumer without saying a word. Except for a few file cabinets, everything else had been moved to the smaller office he'd just left. He had his own thoughts as for why Sebastian had done it, but regardless of why, the larger space was needed. Word of mouth had helped the program, and two more students had signed up, and there were more who wanted to join.

At home they still slept in different bedrooms, and even though they'd discussed changing that while Grandma Mae was in town, they decided against it. When his parents came for dinner, they acted as if things were normal, but as he sat there watching her, he knew no matter how much he wanted things to be as they once were they'd never be the same again. He leaned his left shoulder against the door frame, and waited until she noticed him. He didn't want to disturb the students because the meetings could be intensely private.

She sat in the circle with the kids, and he could tell from the way they listened to her they trusted her. No one interrupted or sat with scowls on their faces. They would probably sit there as long as she asked them, if necessary. When she noticed him, he raised a hand and tapped his watch with his index finger. She glanced at her watch, excused herself from the group and walked toward him.

76

Petite and proud, that's how he used to think of her. He still did, but something had changed in the later years of their marriage, if he was honest. He didn't think she didn't love him, and he knew he loved her, but it wasn't the same.

Something was different.

And not just in her affections for him, but in the way she acted. He watched the sway of her hips and the confidence of her steps and knew she was recapturing some of the spunk he remembered from college. When she reached him, she hugged him and the delicate fabric beneath his fingers only enhanced his memories of her soft brown skin. As she stepped away, he caught a whiff of cucumber, the scented lotion she used on the children and herself. The smell sparked a memory of bath-time with Maddie. He'd forgotten the lotion, and she told him he had to use it on her so that her skin would be like mommy's. After he put it on her, he let her put some on his face and arms. It was one of his happiest memories.

The hug she'd given him was about as much as they ever touched anymore. In front of his parents there was the occasional peck on the cheek, but never anything more intimate. At first he'd wanted it. He'd begged her to return to their bed, but she wasn't ready. And now, after weeks of sleeping apart, it's been accepted by both of them.

He looked down into dark brown eyes filled with knowledge and happiness, and something kicked him in his stomach. There was no love. Not the kind that had lived in those eyes for years. Not the kind that used to fill him up and give him the energy he needed to conquer the world. A smile curved her lips, and it was a sealed. It was the look a friend gives to another. He didn't touch her heart the way it once did.

What was he supposed to do? Give up? He admitted he screwed up. But, now, he wasn't even sure what he wanted anymore. Saving his family was important to him. Having his family, friends, co-workers—everyone!—see him as a man was crucial. What would they think of him, if he left a woman like Rumer for a woman like Gabriela?

She looked over her shoulder at the young men waiting on her return before she spoke. The guys tried to avoid watching them. Their gazes jumped around the room and they engaged each other in conversation, but inevitably, their eyes fell back on them.

"I'm going to be a little late." She smiled again. "We're planning a dinner trip to the harbor." She reached out and placed one of her small hands on his arm. There was a slight squeeze before she let her hand fall. "I will call you when I'm on the way home."

"Okay, I just wanted to make sure." He wanted to do something, but what? "I will see you when you get home."

She turned and walked away to rejoin the men waiting for her. He didn't know what he wanted, but he did know he wanted the pain in his chest to go away. His best friend had just walked away from him, and there was the strong possibility he may never be able to get her to love him again. Not just because he didn't deserve it, but also because there was another man sticking his nose in where it didn't belong.

Chapter Thirteen

Kevin leaned against a wall with his hands folded across his chest. His sneaker covered feet were crossed at the ankle with the sides of his shoes touching his book bag. His normally blond hair was now more of a pink blond Mohawk masterpiece. Rumer rested her butt on the back of one of the chairs in the circle, and reached behind her with both hands to grip the top rim adding support. She didn't want to fall and split her new skirt. She'd received compliments from everyone when she put it on. She was sure Sebastian liked it, too. If the way his eyes followed her when she arrived was any indication.

"What are you doing here so early?" she asked.

She stayed late a few nights with the guys planning an upcoming dinner, so she thought she'd come in early to go over the session for later that day. She was surprised when she glanced up at the knock on the door to find Kevin.

"I don't know." He shrugged his shoulders. "I didn't think you'd be here. I just…"

Kevin didn't talk a lot. He seemed to prefer to listen. But, other boys in the group looked up to him because he didn't hide himself. Some of the young men in the group were not openly gay. But, Kevin was, and they respected him for that. So, did she. She waited to see if he would finish his sentence, but it didn't look like he would.

"You know you can tell me anything. That's what this group is all about," she said, softly.

Kevin's downturned eyes raised and for the first time since he'd walked into the room, he focused on her. "The guy

I'm dating isn't 'out.'" He used his hands to make air quotes, and then folded them back over his chest.

She'd quickly discovered this wasn't uncommon. Her group was almost half and half, and of them most of the guys they were dating weren't out. She hated to hear it because in a short period of time, she'd grown to love each of her boys, and to know that someone out there wasn't loving them in the way they deserved made her want to find each one of them and shake them by the shoulders until they figured it out.

"Okay. What's happening?" she asked because she knew there was more than he was saying.

"His brother." Kevin balled up a fist and slammed it against the wall behind him. "Ms. Rumer his brother is a jerk. He found me on campus and threatened me."

Her heart jumped. "Kevin, do you think he was serious?" She would have to get Sebastian involved. They had a process worked out with the Baltimore Police Department just for cases like this. "We can't take threats lightly."

"I know, Ms. Rumer." He began to nudge his backpack with one of his feet. "But, I'm not scared. I'm not going to let him try to change me. I talked with Gary about it, and he told me he'd smooth everything out with his brother. Tell him we're just friends. We skateboard together and that's it. Nothing else." He stopped kicking the bag and looked at her.

She pushed the chair away, and took a few steps toward him. She placed her hands on his shoulders. "Kevin, this isn't something that we take lightly." When his eyes dropped away, she squeezed his shoulders to get his attention again. "I have to tell them you brought this to my attention. I'm obligated to make sure you're safe."

His shrugged his shoulders in response.

She knew that this young boy, who was taller than her, didn't see himself as a child. He saw himself as a man. And she didn't want to do anything to undermine that. "I know you're strong, and you can take care of yourself, but there's no way I'm going to let you walk out of here today without you filling out the paperwork, so that we can discuss it with our liaison." She squeezed his shoulders again. "Okay." If anything happened to him and she did nothing, there would be no way for her to forgive herself.

"Okay." Some of the anger in his expression was gone. "Ms. Rumer, you're not going to tell the guys about this are you?"

She dropped her hands from his shoulders. She wouldn't tell them, but she would schedule one on ones with each of them to make sure none of them were going through similar things and afraid to mention it. There were some upcoming sessions planned with the Baltimore Police Department, but maybe she needed to move some of those dates up. "Of course not. But you and all of the guys have my cell for emergencies. You know you can use it, if you can't reach me here."

Finally, he smiled. "Yes," he said as he tapped a pocket which looked like it had a phone stuffed in it. "And, Ms. Rumer—"

The other boys began to file into the room creating noise as they dropped book bags and grabbed chairs.

"—thank you," he finished as he reached down to pick-up his own bag and grab a seat.

She glanced at the young men around the room. Various races: black, white, Latino. Some had beards, some didn't. The majority of them had piercings she could see, and she was more than confident others had some she couldn't. There were all body types: short, tall, gym rats, or couch potatoes. Gamers. Future financial gurus. Different ages, but everyone in her group was under twenty-five because her program was targeted for undergraduate college students.

Even if they didn't think so, they were young and vulnerable. They saw themselves as men, not babies. The only thing she wanted to do was figure out how to protect them from the cruel world walking down the street in front of their building. From the street, there was only one small sign on the façade of the building. And after speaking with Sebastian, she knew there was a reason for that. He didn't want to attract unnecessary attention. He compared it to planned parenthood buildings. That comparison had made it click for her.

RUMER

She'd ignored Kevin's world until Luke dropped it into her lap. She didn't know if that made her a good person or not.

But, the love that filled her heart for the young men that had invited her into their lives grew stronger every day. She couldn't disregard it any more.

Gabriela surfed through the movie channels searching for something interesting to watch. Nothing. Or, maybe it was the fact that a month and a half of sitting on her butt because the pain surging through her body made it more comfortable to sit or lie down, instead of moving, had allowed her to watch every single movie ever made.

Her desire to get back to the center to do what she needed to do kept nagging at the back of her mind. She pushed her body too much too fast. She had to come to terms with the fact that her healing wasn't complete and, if she was lucky, it would only take a few more weeks, but it could be months before her body was completely okay.

She'd never thought she would feel disconnected from her new body. But, the pain and slight infection had done just that. The new medications had left her a little more loopy than normal, so, after discussing it with her doctor, she'd decided to stop taking them. He'd argued against it, but with a little more care and time to heal, it'd be fine. She had to take a few more baths than normal, but they helped to take care of other medical nuisances, and what girl doesn't love a long warm bath.

The almost too hot water cocooning her body wasn't scented with any of her much loved bath beads or bubble bath, but it still did the trick. She let her head fall back to rest on the warmed, but still cooler, enamel of the tub. Stretching her legs out and flexing her toes, she thought, one of the first things she was going to do when healthy was go to the salon. Her hands, feet, legs, everything looked a mess. Her mother helped a lot; she'd been too sore and stiff to care about the way she looked.

But her mother hadn't had to do it alone. A few of her friends from the salon had come by, and she was grateful.

They'd plucked, waxed, and painted as much as they could without overwhelming her. And, of course, there was Sebastian. He came by practically every other day, to sit and talk. The only time he disappeared was when she asked questions about the center or, more specifically, Luke.

No matter how many questions she asked, he would only reassure her that he hadn't dug a huge hole somewhere and dropped him in it. That was a good thing. She still knew Sebastian was up to something, but until she went back to work, she wouldn't know what. Because as much as she wanted to know, she refused to speak to Luke herself. She wanted to take the time off to rehabilitate in more than one way. Not just her body, but her heart. When she saw him again, he'd have no choice but to see her as a woman. One hundred percent!

The thought of him ignited flames in parts of her that were still aching and sore. She refused to do any more damage to him or his family. She had never set out to be a woman who didn't respect herself or anyone else. Her heart had simply forced her to ignore every rational thought she had. But, now, away from the source of her confusion, she understood that what she'd done was wrong.

The sounds of Rumer's children crying, and the anxiety she felt for causing Rumer's anger balled into a knot in her stomach. She sat up and leaned her head over the side of the tub. She inhaled deeply allowing the cool air to center her and ease her down from the plateau of panic that seemed to find her more and more.

Twisting her body, she turned on the faucets and placed a hand underneath the spray to test the temperature until she had it just as she wanted it. And she refilled the bath. Then, she loosened her hair from the bun she'd tied the locks of her hair into before the bath, and dipped her whole body under the water.

When she rose again, she was even more convicted to her goal. Get healthy. Get back to work. Find Rumer. Forget...forget about Luke. She fell in love with him; she could fall out of love with him.

Chapter Fourteen

Summer seemed to end a little faster in cities built on the water. The nights were a little cooler, the winds a little stronger. Sebastian didn't mind, not tonight. He'd invited Rumer to discuss Kevin's predicament over dinner, and she'd accepted. Seated on the patio of one of his favorite seafood restaurants, they were surrounded by a delicious mixture of steak and lobster. As the air blew around them, it blew strands of hair across her face creating a tussled look that had him wondering if that's what she'd look like after they'd made love as she lie in his bed naked.

He allowed himself to play with that image in his mind. He took his time skimming his fingers along her warm soft skin, caressing her breasts, tasting her lips, until his desires overtook him. His hands continued to explore her body—

"Sebastian," Rumer said. Her eyes showed concern.

He quickly tried to catch up with what she'd shared with him. Kevin was being bullied by the brother of his boyfriend, and she wanted to know what they could do. He'd discussed everything she'd initially shared with him with BPD, and unfortunately, it didn't seem like there was much that could be done. Not until the jerk had actually made a move. Thoughts of his youth with Gabriela sprung to his mind. Creeps like Kevin's boyfriend's brother were the reason, he'd played bodyguard their whole childhood.

"Rumer, we can try to keep an eye on Kevin." He thought about it more. "Maybe we institute some sort of a buddy program for a while. Get him to make sure he's with at least one other person at all times." He thought about Kevin's reaction. "At least for a while."

"I know he'll think we're treating him like a baby, if we officially call it a buddy program," she responded. She used one of her hands to brush her hair out of her face. A useless effort to control and fight against the wind. Giving up, she rested her hand on the table.

"Maybe we find a different name." He reached out and covered one of her hands with one of his. Her eyes darted to their hands, but she didn't pull away. "Guys his age are almost never alone anyway. I have a great relationship with the college because of the center." He'd made that one of his goals. He never wanted another kid to feel like Gabriela, alienated. "I can have an 'unofficial' conversation with the campus police, but they won't be able to do anything."

She pushed her plate of half eaten food away, but she didn't pull her hand away from his.

That pleased him, too much.

"This is horrible. It's always the same thing. Before you can get any help, you have to have a victim," she said.

He wished he knew what to say to erase the heartbreak in her voice. "Not necessarily someone hurt, but a proven threat. The school cares. Trust me." He squeezed her hand.

Her gaze fell on his. "I guess you've seen a lot, huh?" She paused. "Tell me more about your brother."

He hadn't expected dinner on the waterfront surrounded by food, wine, and music to end up in a discussion about him, and especially not about Gabriela. A part of him welcomed the opportunity to spill everything, and watch Luke go down in flames. But, he wasn't quite sure about what he wanted, yet. The only thing he did know was that he didn't want to risk the possibility of destroying his chances of having another night on the harbor with her.

This time he sat back in his chair. What could he tell her that wouldn't screw everything up for him? Who cared what it did for Luke?

Rumer didn't think she'd even taken a breath while she waited for Sebastian's response. She was about to tell him she didn't mean to pry when he started to speak.

"My brother and I have different fathers. My father was my mother's first love, and she left my brother's father to return to him when we were young. And that didn't help things as a kid." He ran an index finger over the curve of his ear, absently, as he thought. "My father wasn't that accepting of having a son—step-son—that wasn't all man," he laughed, sardonically. "My brother had problems fitting in at school, and switched them a lot. He ran away a few times, and after high school, he left. And for a long time, I only saw him when I went to visit."

"I'm sorry, Sebastian." She had brothers and sisters that she'd never met, and something inside of her still missed them. As a kid, she'd wished for sisters. It's not a lot of fun to be the voice of every doll in the dollhouse. At her wedding, she'd thought, with her father absent, if she'd had a brother, he could've walked her down the aisle. Luke's dad had stepped in and although she loved him for it, it still hadn't been the same.

"Why? You weren't one of the bastards that treated him like he was contagious and beat him every time you saw him, or ignored his tears when he came home crying because you didn't know how to deal." Anger showed in the tight line of his lips and the creases deepening in his forehead.

She gasped audibly. "What about—"

"—our mother. Don't get me wrong, she's wonderful, but sometimes...it's difficult. And that's just it."

Rumer thought that was her. She was like his mother. She didn't understand, and she stood on the sidelines. But, now, things were different, and she wouldn't allow anything to happen to Kevin. She wanted to share the crazy emotions flowing through her, but she didn't want to lose his respect.

"Sebastian," she began, "I never thought I would care as much as I do about these kids, and I've only been here for little more than a month. I don't know how you survived taking care of your brother for so many years without exploding."

He smiled, and the clench in her belly loosened.

"Who says I didn't explode a few times? I just did it my own way."

That made her smile. He'd been through much more than he was telling her, but he still tried to find a way to lighten the situation. Secretly, she wished he'd share more with her about how he coped, but he didn't elaborate, and she moved on. "Didn't you also mention a sister?" she asked.

His expression went blank.

"I'm didn't mean to pry." He shared the story of his brother, and here she was pushing, trying to find out more. She didn't know what made her think she deserved to know so much. She hadn't shared any of her life with Luke, or what originally brought her to the center. Sebastian wasn't dumb; she was certain he knew her marriage had its problems. But, sill, she hadn't personally sat down and laid out the details. It would be nice to talk about it with someone else, but Sebastian ran the center and she didn't want to cause problems for Luke. Sebastian may know Gabriela, and he might be offended by what Luke did. Hadn't he fired one guy for doing something similar, or worse? "Sebastian, you're doing such great work." She extended a hand toward him with the palm up. "I'm sure your brother knows that, and he's proud of you."

Sebastian hesitated, but he placed his hand in hers, and just like the first time, she liked it. A lot! His touch was different from Luke's. Luke had been the only man she'd ever known, intimately. No other man had been able to elicit the thoughts Sebastian could with nothing but a smile and the brush of his hand against hers. The size of his hand swallowed hers as it rested on the table, and its weight: solid and heavy, amped up her curiosity. Would his caresses be gentle and soft, like Luke's, or more possessive and strong?

Nothing was wrong with soft and gentle, but sometimes, she just wanted more. She'd dreamed of Luke claiming her in a way that sexually erased all thoughts of her ever wanting another man. Not that he didn't satisfy her, most times he did. But, the passion she'd hoped would burst into a thousand red hot flames never grew. It had smoldered, and as of late, gone out completely.

She lifted her eyes from their hands and found Sebastian's gaze locked on her. An almost unrecognizable energy created of pure desire coursed through her. She didn't have to take her eyes away from his to check what she already knew, her skin, once again, was covered in goose bumps at the thought of possibly knowing what it would be like to be kissed by Sebastian. To wrap her arms around his neck, allow her hands to play with the dark silky curls of his hair while his mouth explored hers.

Finally, she pulled her hands away, and crossed her legs. She tried her best to shut down her body's reaction to the beautiful man sitting across from her that seemed more than capable of reading the thoughts flashing through her mind.

Chapter Fifteen

For a week, Sebastian had managed to find different reasons to drop by and check on Kevin between classes. He'd even conned Kevin into giving him his weekly schedule. That made it easier to keep an eye on him without him knowing. Because he was a freshman, he lived on campus, so that made it a little easier to watch him, but Sebastian didn't know where his boyfriend lived. This time, he joined Kevin while he walked to one of his classes. It had taken a lot of convincing, but the kid agreed to let him speak with his boyfriend. Days of playing bodyguard and big brother, and he still wouldn't point out the guy's brother. Still, Sebastian knew just by being seen on campus he would place a few second thoughts in the guy's head if the bully saw him.

He'd had a lot of practice in the art of intimidation. Years of playing football, and working out had made him a solid two-hundred twenty pounds, and at six feet three and a half inches in his bare feet, most men thought more than twice before approaching him about anything. And today, he wasn't wearing his smiley face. He was deep in thought about how to protect this kid who meant so much to Rumer and to him. It was beginning to piss him off how much he cared about what did and didn't matter to Rumer. That wasn't part of his plan, but he blew off those thoughts and decided he'd take care of that later, after he helped Kevin.

The boy walking beside him reminded him too much of Gabriela. The strong-willed young man would never back down, and just like Gabriela, he'd end up hurt. He knew it. He didn't want to tell Rumer what clawed at his gut. But from what Kevin shared with him—what the young man wanted to hide, too—he was confident the guy's brother blamed him for changing his brother. How many idiots had said that to him? Some of them even had the balls to show up as his center begging for a fight, and he still had enough of the ball buster in him to give them what they wanted. That was another reason he needed to have a good relationship with BPD, and a good lawyer on retainer.

He scanned the college's campus as they walked. Anyone that paid a little too much attention he etched a sketch of in his head. Because if he'd wanted to intimidate someone, he'd insinuate himself in their path. Make sure they saw him every day coming and going. Let them know that he could get them at any time. He knew the guy causing Kevin all the trouble was right in front of him blending in with the innocents racing across the campus with books and bags trying to figure out what life held for them.

Pain!

But, hell, maybe that was just his life, not theirs.

This campus was probably reminiscent of the type of place Rumer met Luke. College sweethearts. Luke had probably placed himself in her path, but not to hurt her, just to grab her attention. Lately, he'd found himself doing just that. He monitored her group more often; he told her it was to learn more about Kevin. Part of that was true, but also, he wanted to see her. He loved the sound of her voice, and when she was with the boys, she didn't care about anything else. She focused on them and their needs. He loved her passion. He wondered how long had it taken Luke to capture her attention? Her heart? As long as it had taken Luke to break his sister's? How many times had he thought about kicking the man's ass, just like he'd done as a teenager?

Gabriela didn't want him to hurt Luke, and he'd promised he wouldn't. But, now, he wanted to do it for two reasons, two women. And one of them wasn't his to protect. Luke should've been the one protecting her, their children, and their family. If he were married to a woman like Rumer...too funny. He'd never marry. And he'd never have the chance to love a woman like her.

They were about to walk into a huge building on the perimeter of the campus when he saw a tall lanky guy step from beside a tree. With his legs spread and one hand fisted around the strap of a book bag hanging off one shoulder, he glanced at Kevin and then Sebastian. Kevin didn't move a muscle. Pride hit him square in his chest. The young man had known exactly where the bully would be, and he didn't let it bother him. He focused on the brick building in front of him, and kept walking. He draped an arm over Kevin's shoulder, and to the young man's credit, he still didn't stop. But, the slightly older guy dressed in blue jeans and sneakers glared. Another guy, dressed much the same, joined him, and after they exchanged a few words, they turned and walked down a tree lined path in a different direction.

He was sure that dude was the problem. Now, he knew who he was looking for. That was a good thing. Dropping off his cargo at his English class, he sought out to follow the same path his two jean clad friends had just taken.

That night at the center, Sebastian closed the door to his office for one of the first times ever. What was said between the three in the room didn't need to go any further. He'd listened to Kevin explain why he didn't want to take any of their suggestions about taking classes online for a while, or transferring to another campus for a semester. He and Rumer had wanted to give the other kid's brother a little time to cool off. Time to forget about Kevin, and to realize that his brother was who he was, and nothing or nobody would change it.

Kevin, like all males his age, thought that was a coward's way out.

"Kevin, sweetie, we don't want to see you hurt," Rumer said. "And until he actually threatens you in a way we can prove, or he touches you, there's not much we can get campus police to do."

Sebastian didn't say much. He wanted to allow Rumer to lead the discussion because he agreed with Kevin. A couple of boxing lessons, and he was sure the kid would surprise a few people. Gabriela sure as hell did. One day, his sister walked up to him, and said I'm tired of people beating me up. After that, they sparred together on a regular basis. They never told their parents, but he didn't know how else he could help Gabriela. He wouldn't always be there, and he wanted to make sure that when he wasn't there she'd be able to do it for herself. And surprising someone with a clean punch was a great way to do it.

He continued to watch as Rumer tried another tactic.

"Kevin, what if...what if this kid tries to hurt his own brother? He can't run from him like you can?" She turned her chair so that she could face him, and reached for his hands. She held them in hers stroking her thumbs over the back of his hands as his covered hers.

Sebastian remembered how she'd done the same thing to his, and the place where their hands had touched began to tingle. He'd noticed the same thing then as he did now, her hands were so small. So fragile. But, she was the mother of two, and she was about to take on the world to protect this kid that she hadn't even known for two months. Her heart was too big. And Luke had crushed it. A hot spike of pain hit him hard in his gut. Gabriela would be back soon, and if Luke didn't tell Rumer the whole truth, he'd definitely have to do it. He didn't want to be one of the people to cause her any kind of pain.

The knowledge of Kevin's boyfriend not being able to run away seemed to make him more agreeable. "He wouldn't hurt his own brother." The statement seemed to be more of a question.

Rumer glanced toward him. He approached them from where he'd stood leaning his butt against the front edge of his desk.

He didn't have another chair, so he squatted. "Kevin, when people are hateful, we don't know what they're capable of. This guy thinks you 'infected' his brother. He thinks that if you're gone, his brother will be okay. If he can't make you go away, who knows what he will do. Maybe hurting his brother would, in his mind, stop his brother from seeing you."

Kevin's eyes widened. For once, Sebastian saw him as the true innocent he was.

"Why don't we start with just a week," Rumer began, "we'll contact your professors, and get them to allow us to work with you. There has to be a way to work it out."

Sebastian watched Rumer try to squelch a smile. She was beyond happy that Kevin had agreed, but she didn't want him to think she thought he needed protecting or anything. That's why she'd wanted him to be a part of the plan. Because she'd said, "...he was a man men would respect." What did he do to deserve anyone's respect? He fought too much. He drank too much. He wasn't a father. They only thing he'd ever done worthwhile in his life was protecting Gabriela, and sooner or later the two of them would meet, and then what would he do?

His time was running out, and he knew it.

"Kevin, trust me, you're doing the smart thing. This is going to take some time to go away, but it will." He knew it could go away, if they could make the dude forget about Kevin, but if they were too late, and the guy was stuck on getting to him. He didn't know. But, as he sat there with the full understanding that Rumer and Kevin both trusted him to help, he knew he had to find a way to keep the kid safe. "We should still speak with your boyfriend."

"I know I said I would introduce you, but I don't know if he's ready for that," Kevin said.

Rumer squeezed his hands, and said, "We can wait a little while longer on that. But first we need to get things in order with your classes." She gave him a hug as he stood to leave.

He noticed the kid's shoulders didn't seem as tense as they'd been when he'd walked in. At the door, Kevin turned and gave him a slight head nod, he returned it, and the young man was gone leaving him alone with Rumer which wasn't the best idea because daily he became more curious about what it would be like to hold a woman so small and delicate in his arms. To feel her lips on his skin, in so many places. He returned to his desk and his chair. He needed to put some space between himself and her.

He watched as she closed the door and turned to him. Soft black silk fell loosely over her breasts. It rested against her stomach where it met the long grey skirt that hugged her hips and outlined her thighs. The black and white shoes she wore gave her at least another two inches. Sexy and beautiful. The small hunk of metal and wood wouldn't actually stop him, if she ever gave him a signal it was okay to act on what he felt. He didn't know if he was that good of a man. The kind who could respect a woman, and not have sex with her.

She was a woman who'd committed herself to a man who didn't deserve her. Even if he didn't honor his end of the deal, he knew she would. Or, regret it after.

Rumer leaned her back against the door that Kevin had just walked out of. She had no reason to stay behind, but instead of leaving too, she closed it. Sebastian had retreated to his desk, and sat quietly as if waiting on her to say or do something. She didn't think there was anything more they really needed to say, but she didn't want to go. Why? She stood watching him as he watch her, but neither said a word. His gaze roamed her body and, if his eyes were hands, she would've felt his touch on every part of her.

What was happening between them should've scared her, and it did. She glanced at the diamond on her finger. She was a married woman, but it was becoming increasingly more difficult to lie to herself, and mask her attraction to the man who sat on the other side of that desk. She left the safety of her door, and approached him slowly. His soft brown eyes seemed to caution her to stay where she stood, but today, she refused to head the warning, and she listened to the steadily increasing beat of her own heart.

All her life, she'd played it safe, and what had it gotten her. Her husband was in love with another woman, and her life was falling apart. The only thing that made sense was the courage of the man in front of her. He'd protected so many for no reason, but love. And, at her request, he'd taken on the challenge of helping Kevin. God, her mind was working overtime. Because the more she thought about the things Sebastian had endured and what he'd accomplished, she craved more of him. An intimacy she hadn't ever desired from any man, other than Luke.

As she rounded his desk, he pushed his chair back, inviting her, and she could see from the jean covered bulge he didn't hide that he was as affected by her as she was him.

He stood and she didn't know what to do. He covered the distance that separated them in one step.

Big strong hands rested on her hips. His thumbs moved in an up and down motion on her stomach. She couldn't believe how intensely her body had wanted this simple touch from him. Without thinking, she stepped even closer. She could no longer see his face, and had to lean her head back to see his eyes. His features were strained as if he was holding himself back, and she didn't want that. She brushed her breasts against him, and his response was to lower his head. He was about to do it. He was about to kiss her. She hadn't realized how much she wanted this moment, till now. She leaned her head back further to give him full access.

Warm breath brushed across her ear, and she inhaled deeply. Walnuts, she thought. He smelled like nuts and grass. She took another deep breath, and knew she'd never forget that scent.

His lips, soft and warm, touched the curve of her ear. "Rumer...go home."

The breath she'd been holding in anticipation burst from her. She'd been so stupid. Why would a man like him want a woman like her? Not even for a lousy one night stand. She had two kids and was married; he had to have gorgeous women throwing themselves at him every day.

Stupid!

She tried to take a step back, but his hands tightened for a second, holding her in place. His chin slid along the side of her head, and again she felt his lips touch that place on her ear that never seemed so sensitive before. She wanted to run to a corner and hide.

His hands fell from her side, and she turned and practically ran out of the office. She didn't look back because she didn't want to see him laughing at her. How could she have interpreted all the signs wrong? His body wanted her. She knew it. So, why had he rejected her? Because she was short and dumpy, and he didn't want to waste his time. She had to get out of the building before someone stopped her. The tears she held back stung the corners of her eyes. Racing across the parking lot to her car, she popped the lock and dropped into the driver's seat. Only when she'd driven out of the lot and onto the street did she feel safe enough to let the tears fall. She didn't hold back anything. She cried for her dead marriage, her stupid crush, her children, and Kevin. By the time she reached her house, her silk blouse stuck to her chest. Good thing it was black. She hoped no one would notice it was wet.

Even with Grandma Mae's help, it'd taken a long time to put the kids to sleep. At almost eight months, Tyler knew he wasn't in his mother's arms, and fought hard against Luke bedding him down. Maddie flat out refused. Normally, a few books, and she would be out, but that's when she knew her mom was in the house. Not tonight.

He knew Rumer was at the center. He thought she'd be home before now, but her nights had been getting longer and longer. It all felt so familiar. He'd done the same thing with Gabriela. The thought tugged at something inside of him. Gabriela still wasn't answering his calls or texts. As he closed Maddie's bedroom door, he walked down the hall to his room—he and Rumer hadn't shared a bed since his betrayal—he mourned the loss of wife, his best friend.

He heard the garage door, and knew she'd arrived. He gave her time to enter the house and make it to her bedroom before he sought her out. He knocked on her closed door, and when she responded, he walked in. How had they gone from being friends and lovers to being what, roommates? He hated himself for what he'd done to them, and what he was continuing to do to her.

She'd changed into soft cottony pajama bottoms and a tank top. More of the weight she'd gained while carrying Tyler had fallen off, and her hair had grown several inches. How was it possible for her to continue to get more beautiful? But, she was sad. He knew she was dealing with a lot because of Kevin. She worried about him every day. But, this...this was different.

"Rumer, are you okay?" he asked.

Glistening eyes met his. "I'm okay."

He closed the door and padded barefoot across the carpeted bedroom floor toward her. He hesitated. Why? Even if their marriage wasn't what it should be they were friends. He wrapped his arms around her, and he felt her small body tremble. "Tell me."

She leaned her forehead against his chest, and he tightened his embrace when he felt her inhale deeply. She was in pain, and didn't want to tell him. He lowered his head and allowed the side of his forehead to touch the top of her head. The watery fresh scent of cucumber washed over him. "You're my best friend. I love you."

She broke free of his arms and tiny fists pounded his chest as tears fell. He didn't try to avoid or deflect one tiny punch. Her hands fisted the white cotton of his t-shirt, and then she pushed him away and, exhausted, dropped to the bed behind her.

Her gaze locked on his. "Why did you stop loving me?" she asked.

His heart stopped. Is that what she thought? Did she actually think he woke one day and no longer loved her. He had loved her every day from the moment he first saw her. But, when he met Gabriela, he couldn't explain it. A piece of a puzzle he didn't know was missing fell into place. "I never stopped loving you."

"That's a lie," she said through heavy sobs.

"No," he said as he took a few steps and knelt on the floor in front of her. "I don't think I'll ever be able to stop loving you, Rumer. You were my first real love. The mother of my children. I think I was always meant to love you. But—"

"—I wasn't enough for you," she sobbed. "What was missing? What did you need from me?"

He placed his hands on her thighs allowing his thumbs to move up and down as he pondered his words. "There wasn't anything I was aware of." He searched for more. "I think she"—he swallowed—"just awoke something, a passion, I didn't know was missing."

Her tears stopped. "Do you still want her?"

He knew the answer, but he didn't know what reaction his response would get. He didn't know what he wanted for his future. What would his answer mean for his family, his children? "Yes." He fell back onto his butt and waited for her to tell him to pack his bags and get the hell out.

Watery dark brown eyes searched his face. "Am I such a horrible person to spend a lifetime loving?"

He never thought she'd think any of this was her fault, but here she was in front of him thinking that the hell he'd created was, in some way, because of her. He stood and joined her on the bed. He picked her hands up off her lap and held them in his. They were warm. Too warm. As if they channeled all the anger and sadness that couldn't be shown by her tears. He released one of her hands to place his hand underneath her chin to lift her eyes to meet his.

"I don't know if I know how to describe the woman you are. What you've meant to me and my life. I can't see living it without you as a part of it. I guess that's why I wanted to keep you for myself when I don't deserve you." He paused. "But, it's not fair of me to cause you this kind of pain. None of this is your fault."

There was still so much she didn't know. He thought about telling her the whole truth about Gabriela, but the dried tears on her face, the slight tremble of her bottom lip, and the overwhelming sadness pouring from her heart changed his mind. He couldn't cause her any more pain tonight.

Instead, he pulled her to her feet, and guided her to top of the bed. He tucked one more person into bed that night; gently he placed a kiss on her forehead and closed the door behind him. Hidden away in his own room, he threw himself on to the bed and let his anger at himself flow in the only way he could. Hot tears burned as the full weight of understanding what he'd done to Rumer hit him like a punch from a heavy weight boxer square on the jaw.

Chapter Sixteen

A week had passed, and Sebastian didn't know what to do to repair the friendship between him and Rumer. Didn't she know how hard it was for a man like him to refuse an invitation from a woman like her? He had tried to be the best kind of man. His own damn body was angry with him, and showed it to him every night in dreams. Constantly, his mind tormented him with memories of the touch of her skin to his, her scent, and the look in her eyes when he told her to go home.

His phone rang, and he tapped his Bluetooth. The phone connected with his truck's speakers. "Hello."

The voice was one of the customer service reps from his alarm company. They were calling to check on the center. A motion detector had been activated. They'd had problems before with vandals, so he'd upgraded the alarm system. All the doors and windows, except the windows on the third floor were censored.

He asked the guy to dispatch the police, and told them he was in route himself.

Idiot! He cursed through his open driver's side window at the crazy driver hauling ass around the corner as he turned down the street to the center.

He slammed on his brakes as he pulled up to the center. He couldn't get as close as he wanted because of the line of police cars. Blue lights flashed and, in an odd way, gave the building a macabre look. Windows were broken. There was a ladder on the side of the building. The beige brick had been tagged with every stereotypical slur their small brains could think of. They couldn't even be original. Crude pictures accompanied some of the words. The bastards had been smart. He glared at the ladder and he didn't need an explanation.

Damn! He parked the car where it was on the street, and got out running toward the building. He scanned the people hanging out outside the building: the kids, his staff. Where was Rumer?

Finally, he saw her. There was a blockade of police between him and her; he slowed, but he wasn't stopping. One of the cops he knew saw him coming, and raised the yellow tape that he would've broken through as he headed toward her. When he was within reach, he didn't care who saw him, he pulled her into his arms, not because she was hurt, but because he wanted to protect her.

She didn't fight his hold. After a minute or two, he noticed that people were trying to divert their eyes from them. He released her, but he placed a hand on each arm, and gazed down at her. "Are you okay?"

"Yes, I wasn't inside." She glanced over her shoulder at the building. "No one was. It was like this when we all arrived." She placed her hands palm down on his chest. "I'm sorry this happened to your beautiful building."

He looked at the building, then her, and the people around them. "As long as you're okay." If the punks had done this while she was in the building, he wouldn't have been responsible for his next move. After reassuring himself that she was okay, he turned to go speak with one of the officers to find out who was in charge.

Hours later, Sebastian stood in the center of his office barely able to control his anger. The punks who'd vandalized the center had done damage on every floor. They weren't there to steal, but to damage. They'd smashed computers, spray painted walls, and busted furniture. The cops said it must've been quite a few of them because of the level of damage. He'd thought the damage had been done over night, but according to his alarm company and the police they'd broken in not long before the staff arrived. The police had said their response time had been less than fifteen minutes.

Fifteen minutes!

He bent over to pick up his desk when he felt someone enter his office. He turned and found Rumer hovering at the door. He focused on the broken pieces of the desk again because he needed something to drag his attention away from her.

He'd sent everyone home, and told them he'd call them when things were in good enough order for them to return.

"Are you okay?" she asked.

No. He didn't have the energy to do what he needed to do and fight his attraction to her. "Rumer, you should go home, too."

He heard her release a long exhale. Then he heard the click of her heels against the tiled floor of his office as she approached him. "Sebastian, you don't get to send me home again."

He turned and stared into eyes that, if he could have his way, he'd want to wake up to them every day. He grabbed her wrist and dragged her behind him till they reached the front of the building. He opened the door, and said, "Go home."

She snatched her arm from him, and folded them just below her breasts. "No."

He closed the door, and reached for her. She took a step back. He followed her. She avoided a few pieces of broken crap on the floor, and ended up with her back flat against a wall in the hall way leading to the small cafeteria.

He didn't stop. He placed his hands, palm down, on the wall beside her, encasing her between his arms. He looked down at her, and she didn't draw back. Everything in him wanted to feel her lips against his. His body responded to the nearness of her. To close the gap between them would take nothing. He could lift her up tear away her skirt, and have his dreams become a reality. Certain that she would accept him, and not push him away, he allowed his head to dip, and he nuzzled the side of her neck.

That cucumber scent he hadn't been able to erase from his mind had haunted him in his dreams. It wrapped around him, and he let the fingers of his right hand trace the line of her neck wishing it was his tongue. He wanted so badly to give himself permission to take advantage of what she offered him. He took another long deep inhale before he thrust his fingers into the hair at the nape of her neck and angled her head.

Her eyes locked on his. He knew she wanted him to kiss her. But, he fought the desire that screamed through every muscle of his body.

"Rumer, until you and Luke," he paused as he checked himself for mentioning Luke's damn name, "work things out one way or another, we can only be colleagues and friends."

The haze that clouded her eyes dissipated and her focus became clear. The softness that welcomed him disappeared, and she broke free from his hold with a force he didn't realize her tiny body had.

"So, all of this teasing me was some sort of a game for you." She stomped toward the door he'd just told her to leave through. "It's just your way of having fun with the sad 'almost divorcee.'"

"No, any other time, I would've taken you up on the offer." Every time he could. "But, there is a lot going on...with you, the center, me. We both need to get some things worked out."

"Men!" she disappeared through the door before he could say anything else.

He thought that maybe he should follow her, but hell, if he did, and she was still willing he wouldn't be able to say no, twice.

He pulled his cell phone from his pocket and sent a text. When I think you're ready for me, I'll come to you.

He didn't expect a response, but at least she would know. He wanted her. He stuffed the phone back into his pocket and headed back toward his office. He had a cleaning crew coming in the morning, and had a security team watching the building tonight. But, he still wanted to take care of a few things before he left.

He walked into Rumer's meeting room, and read the scrawl on the wall.

Kevin come out, come out, wherever you are.

The bastards had been watching him alright. They'd followed either him or Kevin, and they'd lead them right to Rumer. She didn't know it, but he'd had a conversation with Luke, and told him he'd take full responsibility for their security. Luke had okayed the private patrol he'd put on their house. He'd done the same with Kevin. Kevin had been staying with his parents off campus till things cooled down, but it looks like the perverts were getting tired of waiting for him to return. And after what happened to the center Kevin was ready to return and face them.

The kid had wanted to go and pay them back for what they'd done to the center. He'd worried about Rumer, too. It was the first question the guy had asked him.

He smiled. How'd she managed to make three men fall in love with her? No matter what he felt about Luke, the prick had asked him to tell Gabriela not to return to the center till they got everything straightened out. He gave him credit for caring at least that much. Even if he didn't deserve either of them.

He stripped off his shirt because he didn't want any of the paint remover to fade the fabric. He dipped the sponge into the solution and swiped it across the wall over and over until the words began to fade away.

When he was satisfied, he tossed his shirt over his shoulder, and left the center. In the lot, he paused at his car. He memorized every broken window, every hateful word, and then he slid into his car and drove away.

How could kids have so much anger in them that they were willing to destroy and hurt others? He'd started the center because of the pain he'd watched Gabriela experience as a child. Because he saw how much his father had wanted to love her, but was afraid to, and how confused their mother seemed by it all.

Rumer had entered the doors of the center with that same confused look in her eyes, but unlike his mother, her eyes no longer held that same distant almost detached gaze. The tears she held back when he found her outside of the building that morning were genuine. What her husband had coaxed her into doing because he wanted to try to save their marriage, and convince himself and her that he wasn't gay had exposed her to something she wasn't comfortable with. But, she wasn't running from any of it, from him.

His hands tightened on the steering wheel.

She wasn't running from him!

Chapter Seventeen

Rumer allowed the weight of everything that happened over the past days to sink in. Luke had admitted he loved another woman in a way he no longer loved her. Sebastian rejected her. Vandals destroyed the center which had been a haven for so many.

Ty's small head rested on her arm as she cuddled him a little closer to her breasts. As normal, after he'd fed, his eyelids had gotten heavier and heavier until, no matter how hard he fought sleep, he couldn't keep them open. She closed her own eyes, and rested her head on the cushion of her chair. She wasn't sleepy, but holding him was peaceful. The musical carousel and Ty's warmth grounded her.

What would she have done if she'd come home to find the house where she raised her children destroyed? To have someone violate something so personal and important would crush her. Her heart broke all over again for Sebastian. His expression had been unreadable. Only when he'd held her did she feel his concern for her pour from his body into her. She'd hated the moment he pulled away. But, she knew it'd been the right thing to do. People were openly gawking, they knew her husband. Did they also know he loved another woman?

And later, Sebastian wouldn't allow her to comfort him. She'd left angry because he'd dismissed her again. Then she'd read the text, and it made her forgive everything. Because, she realized, he was giving her time. Time to make a decision about her marriage. Her husband. He knew she and Luke had problems with their marriage, but he'd never asked her what or why. He knew she hadn't come to the center "out of the goodness of her heart." She'd come because Luke had asked.

RUMER

What must Sebastian think of people like her?

But, now, she did care, and she would've given anything, if he'd have allowed her to be the woman he gave his confidence. The person he turned to in the middle of the night when he couldn't sleep. The woman who shared his wildest fantasies and biggest regrets.

She opened her eyes at the squirm of her son's tiny body. Pushing up from the chair with one hand, she cradled him in the other arm. Briefly, his eyes opened before closing again. She placed him into this crib, and softly kissed him on the cheek.

She checked on Maddie before she headed to her bed. With one arm bent and resting by her head and the other lying along the length of her body, Maddie softly snored. Her grandmother's door was closed, and there was no light at the base. Good, she thought. Her grandma Mae had been so worried about her when she'd told her and Luke of the break in. Sebastian had called to tell Luke some of the details. Although she'd stormed out of the center, he'd still cared enough to call and talk with Luke.

Soft familiar music seeped from underneath Luke's door. She knew it to be his thinking music. Whenever he had a problem he thought needed solving, he'd play that jazz CD over and over until he had a mental breakthrough of some kind. There was a time when she tired of hearing it. As she stood on the outside of that door trying to remember the last time she'd heard it, she realized it was only a short while ago when she'd heard that song over and over again from his office. Acceptance of what that meant hit her hard. That must've been when he'd met and dated Gabriela.

Every time he played that CD, he was trying to decide what to do about his future, their future. For months, he'd been tormenting himself. He hadn't wanted to hurt her; he'd feared for himself, and had been lost and confused.

How had all these people around her been dealing with life and the world as it is today, while she'd been shielded from it all? She'd allowed herself to be taken care of by others for too long. Her grandmother. Luke. And now, Sebastian. She didn't need them to hide the big, mean, cruel world from her.

She could take care of herself. Sebastian had said he'd come to her when he thought she was ready for him. She hadn't even filed divorce papers because she was too busy pretending with Luke. No arrangements had been made for the house, the children. Nothing.

He'd been right. She wasn't ready.

As Luke's CD continued to play softly in the room behind her, she continued to her room, and closed the door behind her. There was a lot that needed to be done. She needed to talk to her grandmother. To Luke.

When they had everything set and done, then she'd wait. And if Sebastian didn't come to her, she'd find him. But, first, they had to get the center cleaned up, and make sure Kevin was okay.

She hadn't wanted to mention it to Sebastian, her stomach twisted in knots again, she flipped over onto her side and curled up in a ball, she was convinced that this had something to do with Kevin and the boy from his school.

Nothing had been stolen according to the police, and from what she saw before Sebastian had stolen her ability to think, everything seemed smashed and broken, but not a regular robbery. At least, not what she thought would be a normal break-in.

Sebastian had told everyone to stay away for a week. He'd promised he'd contact Kevin, and would take care of everything. She trusted him, but still she wanted to call Kevin and make sure he was okay without scaring him. She pulled her knees up tighter and decided to leave it to Sebastian until she knew more herself.

Allowing her mind to be flooded by the sensations of Sebastian's touch, she relaxed a little, and gave into the strong overwhelming desire to sleep. She'd call Sebastian in the morning to make sure he didn't need her help with anything.

She might not be ready for him, but that didn't mean she couldn't stand beside him until she was. And she would every day. He always took care of everyone else. Who cared for him? Would he allow her?

Chapter Eighteen

Sebastian had teams of cleaners and painters working overtime on the center. He battled against two clocks: the people who needed the center and Gabriela. She refused to listen to him and take more days off. The time it took to have the center repaired after the idiots had broken in had cut out days he'd planned to spend with Rumer. Days he'd hoped to be able to explain who Gabriela was to him.

He checked every room of the center inch by inch because he didn't want one person to see one thing that he'd missed. Not a slur, a picture, a broken chair, or smashed computer. The center was supposed to be a place where people could feel safe and protected, and a bunch of punk kids had managed to change that for everyone.

The police weren't able to tell much from the video because they'd been smart enough to cover their faces and wear gloves. But, he hadn't been able to erase that damn car that had almost side-swiped him out of his head. A junker. The kind of car a college student would drive unless they had a parent footing their bill. The security cameras had caught four guys dressed in dark jeans, hoodies, and masks.

He had no proof other than the tag on Rumer's wall. Their ego wouldn't let them leave without letting someone know it was them. It wasn't enough for the cops, but it was enough for him. He'd spent the weekend on a ride-along with some friends who worked for the college's campus police. There was nothing he could do, if he saw them. But, he wanted to get an idea of who the other guys were. Who had the balls to invade his center? He walked into his office and the smell of fresh paint slapped him in the face. Instead of throwing boring beige back on the walls, he went with a green that gave the room more character. He left his office and headed down the hallway toward Rumer's meeting room. He'd been direct in telling the painters to match the yellow, perfectly.

Hell, if Gabriela showed up before he had the chance to speak with her, she may never see it, but he wanted things to be as normal for her as possible. It wasn't necessarily a good thing, but he was used to fighting. Rumer wasn't. Walking to the wall, he placed his hands on the spot where the warning had been left for Kevin. He touched his fingertips to the yellow paint, and thought, not a trace. People can always try to kill something, but if the Kevins and Gabrielas of the world kept living their way, no one would be able to stop them, including creeps like these bastards.

The vibration of his phone in his pocket pulled his attention away from the freshly painted wall. He read the display. Gabriela.

"I need you to stay away from the center for a few more days," he said. She kept refusing, but he needed her to listen to him for so many reasons that he hadn't shared with her.

"No," she began, "You keep telling me to stay home and heal. I'm much better. Besides, I'll just be sitting in my office." She exhaled loudly. "I should be there with you."

"I can handle this alone. And you're already hurt. I don't want you here closing up or opening early and running into these guys." He hoped she'd listen this time. "I need to focus on helping the police catch these guys. I can't really do that if I'm worried about you."

"You don't have to worry about me—"

"—yes, I do. If they show up again, and you can't run or get away...I won't be able to handle that." If they hurt her, the police would be after him, instead of them.

"Sebastian...you can't keep trying to protect me," she said.

He thought his words were finally getting through to her. He did want to protect her, but he also wanted to protect Rumer. He needed time to be able to figure out how to handle both of them and Luke. His own heart was tied up in this crazy mess, too; he could no longer deny it. But, he'd have to deal with that after everything else, including getting the cowards that bust up the center. "I love you, and I can't worry about you getting hurt. These guys are still out there, and they want Kevin. That's not going to happen." Because he would protect the kid no matter what. "Just a few days. Let us open the doors and see what happens, if everything looks okay then I'll give you the okay."

"Okay. Just a few days, Bastian." She paused. "This was our fight. You did all of this for me, and I won't let you hide it from me. It's my fight, too."

"I know." It was her fight, too. But, that didn't mean he'd allow her to walk into trouble. She'd be vulnerable if the idiots decided to come back. She always arrived early and stayed late to be there as much as she could for everyone. If she'd been there the other day, they would've probably attacked her. He knew she would've gotten in a few good punches, but not enough against four pricks. "We fight together, but I can't have you injured. You're still healing." He heard something behind him, and turned. "I love you."

"I love you. Bye," she said.

He barely heard her as he ended the call and shoved the phone into his pocket. The woman framed by the door made it difficult for him to concentrate. Bouncy black curls framed her face. A beautiful yellow dress clung to her body in all the right places. At her neckline the fabric folded and draped in such a way that that it gave the illusion of full heavy breasts. Funny how a dress could do that. Or, maybe it was just his imagination going into overdrive because he hadn't seen her in a week, and every part of him was upset about that.

Rumer had hoped to get to the center before anyone else had arrived. She should've known Sebastian would be there in her meeting room. She'd love to imagine he was waiting on her. Dark jeans clung, just right, to his muscled thighs, and the red t-shirt accentuated his tanned skin perfectly. If she hadn't known he pitched in with the cleaner and painters to do a lot of the work himself, she would've sworn he'd been on a beach somewhere vacationing. Well that knowledge and the dark circles underneath his eyes. The warmth of his smile claimed her.

What would it be like to feel his passion? The thought burst into her mind.

She tried to still her need, and squelch her desire to go to him and fold her body around his. They hadn't spoken since the day she'd stormed out of the center.

She tried to shake off the sting of the words she'd heard as she entered the room, "I love you." Who had he been speaking with? She had no right to care. But, that didn't make it any less painful. She'd taken the time away to research lawyers and talk things over with her grandmother. Depending on what happened with the center, and how much, if anything, Sebastian could up her stipend, she and the kids may have to move in with grandma Mae until she found a position flexible enough to fit around the kids' schedule. Nothing had been discussed with Luke because she wasn't quite ready to fully admit her marriage was over. But, standing there wanting the man leaning against the wall in front of her to come to her and kiss her, pushed away her doubts.

"I'm sorry. Did you need to finish your call?" She paused. "I can wait for you down the hall." She took a step back to leave.

"What are you doing here so early?" he asked.

"I wanted to talk to you." She rallied her nerve. "I...I'd been thinking about what you said." How was she supposed to say what she really wanted? It didn't seem possible. "I want to help you with all of this." She waved her hands in the air. "I can't just sit by and let you do everything."

"It's not your fight," he said. His tired brown eyes watched her as she approached.

She raised a hand and touched it to his arms. The firm muscle beneath her fingers didn't surprise her. She imagined what it would feel like to be held in his arms as she slept. To have him hold her while he made love to her. The thoughts excited her body in a way that sensitized her nipples and warmed her in the most delicate areas. The soft cotton of her dress had felt soft and sensual against her skin when she'd first slipped it onto her body. But, now the fabric seemed rough, almost abrasive in some areas.

"Sebastian, it may have started off as your battle, but I'm a part of it now. " She let the hand on his arm fall. But, he caught her hand in his and held it against the firmness of his thigh. That ignited even more thoughts of what it would mean to have an intimate touch from this man. "Sebastian, what did you mean by when I'm ready?" Now, she had the nerve because her body ached for him in a way that wouldn't allow her to walk away without asking.

Surprise showed in his expression. "Rumer, there's a lot you don't know about me. And you're still married."

"We were working on our marriage, but," she hated admitting out loud that her marriage had failed, but it needed to be said, "I guess sometimes people grow apart."

"Do you think you are ready to move on?"

She knew it. But, she wanted her children to be prepared for it. They wouldn't see their father every day. "I'm concerned about our children, not me."

"What are you going to do?"

"I have my grandmother, and I'm working on it." She, reluctantly, slid her hand from his and walked to the window beside him. Placing her hands on the windowsill, she leaned forward a little and glanced out the window. Sometimes Baltimore could be so beautiful. Not many cities had rows and rows of old brownstones and cobblestone streets. "I've loved Luke for a long time." She took a chance and glanced at him. "If he hadn't stopped loving me, I don't know..."

"So, you would've stayed with him forever." He turned to lean his left shoulder against the window. He let the fingers of his right hand play with the curls of her hair where they rested on her neck. "Why are you talking to me, then?"

She mirrored his pose, but with her right shoulder against the glass. "I'm not on the rebound, if that's what you mean." She'd been in a sexless marriage for months. They'd gone from lovers to roommates. Both of them had just been too afraid to move on because of what it would mean.

"How do you know?"

Her heart and body had told her a long time ago, but her head ignored them both because she'd wanted to do what she thought was right for her family. But, what she'd realized is that there was no way for her to do what she needed to for her kids, if she wasn't happy. "He loves someone else. He has for months." She hoped she didn't sound pathetic. "He met her here."

His body tensed. Maybe he'd always known, but felt sorry for the poor dumb wife trying to save her marriage, and didn't want to say anything.

"Did you know?"

He didn't respond.

"The woman approached me while I was with my kids, and showed me proof of their relationship." She thought back on the anger she tried to hide from her kids, but they both knew their mommy wasn't happy. If she couldn't fool them now, how'd she ever think she'd be able to keep up the lie forever?

"She approached you." He stopped tugging at the curls of her hair.

"I was with my kids." She placed her left hand on his chest. "I couldn't believe he'd betrayed me by loving someone else. It's the reason he wanted me to work here," she admitted.

"He wanted you to meet the woman?"

"I don't know if he thought all that out. She told me she worked at a nail salon. Luke had told me he'd worked with her, but he never intended to fall in love." The words still hurt, even if she was doing the exact same thing.

"What would you do if you met her?"

"Then or now?" She didn't know what she'd do, if she met the woman some day in the future, but then she would've been ready to confront her and told her to leave her man alone.

"Now."

"I don't know." She really didn't know. It wasn't necessarily about her marriage any longer, but more about

116

the woman being the catalyst for why her life changed. If she'd never come into their lives, maybe she and Luke would still be blissfully ignorant and happy.

"I think you and Luke still have a lot to talk about."

"So, what does that mean?" She had no idea what he was thinking because he wasn't telling her anything.

He placed his hand over the hand resting on his chest. "It's not my place to interfere with your marriage."

"What do you mean? Interfere?" She pulled her hand away. "Do you know something? Did you already know why I came here to work?"

"Yes."

"Yes." She moved away so that she could see his face without being distracted by the closeness of him. "What does that mean? How much did you know?"

Long tense seconds passed before he responded. "I'll answer your questions, but can you handle it?"

How could she respond to that? She didn't know what he knew, but it was clear that he'd answer any question she asked of him. "Did you know he cared about someone else?"

"Yes."

"You know her?"

"Yes."

She knew his answer would be yes. She knew it. Why did she ask? God, she had to be the dumbest woman in the world. How did she keep sticking her foot in her mouth? Glancing at her reflection in the window, she had to stifle the angry laugh bubbling inside of her. Wasted hours had been spent searching for the perfect outfit. And the curls, it'd taken her forever to get the curls to bounce like she'd wanted. Every single thing had been planned, except for being prepared to hear that Sebastian knew and protected the person Luke had cheated on her with the entire time. She'd assumed Sebastian may have seen or known of her, but for him to confirm he knew her stung more than she'd thought it would.

"So, what was all of this? Where you just playing with me to hurt me?"

"No." He paused. "I didn't like what I thought Luke was doing, and I wanted to kick his ass, but I never wanted to hurt you." He took a step, but stopped.

"Did the two of you plan this together in some way? Why would you want me here in your center, if you knew my husband cheated on me with someone here?"

He didn't respond, again.

"Tell me why!" she screamed. Anger pushing hot tears to her eyes. But, something deep in her gut wouldn't let her cry. "Why?"

He'd been open and willing to tell her everything, but he wouldn't answer this last question. Understanding hit her hard. "You know her, personally? She's not just someone who showed up here one day." She knew she was right, even if he didn't answer. "You know her, and she's more important to you than me." Okay, so they hadn't said that whatever it was between them was anything, but it was. "This woman stole Luke from me, and she has you, too."

"Rumer,"—he walked toward her—"calm down." He reached for her, but she wouldn't let him touch her.

"Why is this one woman more important to both of you than me?" Maybe she still wasn't' ready for him. She'd fantasized about coming to him in the center, and having a heart to heart, and then he'd admit he desired her the same way she did him. They'd kiss, finally, and after everything finalized with her divorce, they could be together. But, no. Instead, he was telling her the same thing Luke had.

She didn't matter. The only person who mattered was the other woman, Gabriela.

"Rumer, you're asking me to tell you something that's not my place to tell, but is my place to protect."

"What does that mean?" Him and his stupid sense of duty. What about protecting her? God, could somebody care about her for once? She was trying to be the supportive little wife for Luke, and the "I'll wait for you woman" for Sebastian, but what was either man doing for her?

It's not possible to be the wife of one man, and love another.

"Both of you have been keeping secrets from me. You two have let me walk around here like I'm making a difference. But, really I didn't, not to either of you. Not enough for you or Luke to confide anything in me. To trust me, but you both want me to trust you."

"Rumer."

She pushed past him, and headed toward the door. "No. No more. I'm tired of both of you treating me as if I was a child. I'm not. I'm a woman whose family is falling apart." She pointed at him. "And who obviously has the worst taste in men. And I'm tired of it."

Grabbing the stair rail with him trailing behind her, she ran down the stairs as fast as she could. Stupid high heels!

"Stop following me. I'm leaving. I'm tired of both of you acting like I'm a child."

"Rumer, you're going to fall and break your neck."

She slowed down because he was right, but she still didn't want to deal with him. She stopped at the door with her back to him. He stopped, but she could feel the heat of him, and a small part of her wanted to stay and let him catch her. "Don't touch me." She looked over her shoulder at him. "You told me you'd come to me when I was ready. Maybe that should've been the other way around. I've been honest with you. But you...you've been lying to me since the first day I walked through this door." She swung the door open, and exited. He didn't follow her, and that stung a little.

Chapter Nineteen

Furious, Rumer stomped across the asphalt toward her car. How could everyone think she was such a child who couldn't handle anything? She was a grown woman, and she hadn't considered herself a child since the day her father left her with her grandmother and never returned. So much anger pumped through her that she wished she had a bag to punch or a ball to kick. She heard her name and turned in the direction of the voice.

"Mrs. Wilson?" the voice was filled with surprise.

Rumer's keys fell to the ground. Gabriela! "What are you doing here?" She bent over to retrieve her keys.

"What are you doing here?" The woman moved slowly, and checked the building behind her.

"Are you here looking for my husband?" She didn't owe this woman anything, but Gabriela owed her a lot. "He's not here." And stop hunting down me and my family.

"No. I'm not here for Luke." She checked over her shoulder again. "I'm looking for Bastian."

"Bastian." She'd never called him Bastian. "Why are you looking for him? My husband not enough for you?" Who cared how it sounded? Every which way she turned this woman was there. She was sick of it.

"Mrs. Wilson, I'm sorry." Gabriela's voice wavered. "I didn't mean to hurt your or your family."

Rumer had had enough. "You knowingly chased after a married man." She dragged herself closer to Gabriela. "What do you mean you never meant to hurt my family? My children cried the day you approached me." Her mind was racing. "My husband...my husband and I we haven't been a family since the day you approached me at the grocery store." He hadn't tried to touch her, and except for that first night, she hadn't tried to entice his touch. Quickly checking through her emotions over the past two months, she'd literally been on a roller coaster, emotionally speaking, but it hadn't been his touch she craved. "You destroyed everything—"

"—Rumer, stop it!" Sebastian yelled. His face showed a mixture of too many emotions as he stalked across the lot, and stood between the two women. "Gabby what are you doing here?"

Rumer didn't give her time to answer because she didn't care why she was there, only that she was. And that Sebastian knew her. Why did his voice sound so filled with concern for Gabriela?

"So, you do know her." She jabbed a fisted hand through the air at Gabriela. "Gabby." Rumer's tears fell fast and heavy.

"Rumer," he began, "Gabby is my sister."

"Sister, the one you wouldn't tell me about." She tried to think. "My husband had an affair with your sister. But, he said that she was...she was—"

"—my brother I told you about."

Gabriela walked toward him, and wrapped an arm around his. They were almost the same height and complexion. Sebastian's hair was straight while Gabriela's was filled with thick dark waves. Sebastian's thick muscular body overpowered Gabriela's leaner sinewy frame. They didn't resemble, much. But, their eyes. Intense soft brown. Her husband had fallen in love with his sister, and Sebastian wanted to watch her run around like an idiot until she figured it out. She had been nothing but part of a game for Sebastian. Some cruel sense of payback. He'd practically admitted it to her. He would do whatever it took to protect his brother. And since he hadn't beaten Luke to a pulp in the parking lot, he'd done the next best thing make his sad little housewife fall for him.

Tears poured from her eyes with such force she could barely see. It looked like Gabriela attempted to leave Sebastian and walk toward her, but Sebastian pushed her back, and approached her himself.

"Rumer, I should've told you. The other day when we were here at the center, I should've told you."

"But"—she heaved—"you didn't because it was more fun to watch me walk around like a foolish high school girl with a crush. And you get to watch Luke squirm while he tries to figure out when you would tell me the truth about Gabriela." She leaned to the left to look around him at the woman who had changed her life. "Why did you both do this to me?"

She hadn't seen him close the gap between them, when he touched her, startled, she slapped him. Turning away, she spoke, "I never want to see you again. You've had your fun. I hope you're happy." She paused at her car and glared at Gabriela. "I'm divorcing Luke, you're welcomed to him."

She slammed her door, and pulled away. The last thing she saw was Gabriela wrapping her arms around Sebastian in her rearview mirror. Her grip tightened on the wheel, and she stepped a little harder on the gas. She wished she'd never met either of them; she'd wished the same for Luke, if he wasn't the father of her children.

"Bastian," his sister said, softly, "what's going on? Why was Luke's wife here?"

He stepped away from his sister, and stared in the direction of Rumer's car. The tears in her eyes cut through him; he didn't know if there would ever be any way anyone could squelch the ache that increased with the distance between them. Gabriela deserved answers, too, but everything in him wanted to jump into his car and chase after her. He had no idea where she was headed. Best guest was home, but he didn't know if she'd want her children to see her in the condition she was in when she left. He retrieved his phone from his pocket, and dialed her number. He didn't expect her to answer, but he wanted her to know, if she would allow him, he'd explain it all.

Damn. Why did he wait so long? She'd been right. Initially, he'd wanted to "win" her away from Luke. Let the bastard squirm. He never wanted to hurt her, but he did. Hell, half of him agreed with her. He may be worse than Luke. He knew the truth about everything and everyone. Luke hadn't been told the whole truth, but he still gave into his desire for another woman. But Rumer...she'd been the most innocent of them all, and used by everyone. By Luke to prove he was straight. By Gabriela who wanted her boyfriend. And by him to get even with Luke.

They'd all hurt her.

As he expected, she didn't pick up. The pain knotting up his gut spread through every muscle. He was so wired up, and there wasn't anyone to punch. No one but him. If he knew how to black his own eye, he would. He stared into his sister's eyes. Rumer had needed him just as much as Gabriela had for years, but he hadn't protected her. She hadn't ended up beaten and bloodied because he didn't do what he needed to, but she'd still been hurt, and by him.

"Bastian, tell me what's going on," his sister had more of a demand in her voice.

The center's employees had begun to arrive. Excited voices blended and became indistinguishable as more and more people arrived. Add that to everyone's excitement at Gabriela's return, twenty minutes passed before they were alone again, and could continue their conversation.

Alone in his office, he laid out all the details for Gabby, and for the first time ever, he thought he saw real disappointment in his sister's eyes. Perfectly pruned brows bunched right above the bridge of her nose. Eyes decorated with soft shades of gold and burgundy, which matched her long sundress, drilled into him.

"Bastian, how could you?" She rocketed from her chair, and tossed her purse where she'd sat. The fabric of her dress floated around her with her movements. "None of this was her fault. It was mine. Luke was as innocent as her, but still he and I hurt her. And you...you why did you get involved." Her body trembled from her anger.

He didn't miss the accusation in her tone. "Luke needed to be taught a lesson." When he started the whole crazy thing, he thought of her more as collateral damage. "I wasn't trying to hurt her. He came into this place—our place—and changed things."

"Bastian, maybe it's time for us to adjust a few things." She walked toward him. "You asked me to come back because you started this center and wanted me to help. I returned for that, and also because I missed you and mom, and even your crazy dad. But, maybe I shouldn't have." Her back curved, slightly, from the force of her exhale.

"No, you should be here. We're family." She never should've left. Their parents—he—never should've allowed it. She may have been of age, but it was because the family was so crazy, and Gabriela hadn't believed everyone loved her and wanted her to be a part of the family.

"Yes, but you still think you have to take care of me, and you don't." She placed a hand on his arm. "Big brother, I've been taking care of myself for years."

He dragged a chair from behind his desk, and sat. "I know, but I don't want you to ever think you're alone."

"I know I'm not alone." She leaned a thigh against the front edge of his desk. "But, sometimes I want something that's all mine. Luke wasn't mine. It was wrong," she whispered, "but I know he cared for me." She paused. "And you deserve to have something that's yours. Are you attracted to her? She's beautiful."

He leaned back in the hard plastic chair, and an image of her in that yellow dress flashed in his mind. Attracted barely began to cover the crazy emotions that ran through him when he thought of her. Hell, as he sat trying to explain himself to his sister, his body wanted him to get up, and drive until he found her. He didn't even know where to search, but at least he could do something other than sit.

"I don't know how it happened," he admitted.

She shifted and sat on the top of the desk near his chair. The new desk was an exact match for the old one. In fact just about all the furniture had been easy enough to replace. The insurance company didn't drag their heels, and donations poured in when the story hit the news. It hadn't been as hard as he'd thought to get things back in shape. They had enough money in the bank that he'd thought he could offer Rumer more to come in and work the program on a full-time basis. At least for a year maybe two, if he watched the budget.

The only thing that clawed at his gut was the nagging feeling that sometimes publicity just wasn't a good thing. Now, more fanatics were aware of the center. He'd already contacted the security he hired, and told them he'd continue his contract with them through the top of the year.

"Aren't we something." She laughed. "So, what are we going to do?"

"I don't think there's anything I can do." He was more than positive Rumer would never speak to him again. Her shoulders had trembled from the force of her sobs. Guilt slammed him right in the center of his chest. Using the heel of his hand, he tried to massage the pain away. "How do you get someone to forgive you for using them as a pawn in a chess game?"

"I think we start by giving Rumer a little time, and then we both apologize to her." She paused. "She may not want to hear it, and we'll have to accept that. At least I do." She bumped a knee against the arm of his chair. "You, well, she just may forgive, but you have to give her a reason to want to forgive you."

"And what about you and Luke?"

"There is no me and Luke. There never should've been. If they divorce, and he still thinks there is something between us, maybe then, but not now." She paused. "He has to be willing to accept all of me. And I don't know if he ever will."

She pasted a smile on her face, but she didn't have to say how much is pained her to hope they would divorce, or how much she wished he could forgive her lie, and love her. It was a twisted kind of wish. He stood and pushed the chair away. "You haven't been here in two months. Let's walk you through and back to your office." She hadn't said she was in any kind of pain, and the last few times he'd visited her, he could see a visible change in her attitude. But, he didn't want her to push herself. "Plus I don't want you or anyone else blaming me if you have a relapse of some kind."

She did a twirl before she spoke, "I wouldn't look this gorgeous, if I didn't feel great."

He hugged her. "I'm glad you're better. I'm glad you're back."

"I love you, too." With a playful smile, she pushed him away.

"Okay, okay. Let's go." He stopped. "Give me a sec."

He slid his phone from his pocket, and typed a text, and hit send.

She knows. Find her.

The "I'll kill you, if you hurt her more," didn't need to be said.

Whether or not Rumer forgave him would probably come sometime around the next ice age; but, no other woman had ever come close to making him think about the possibilities of a future like she did. Like his sister, he could be patient.

Chapter Twenty

Luke explained everything to grandma Mae, and jumped in his car. He hadn't realized until he parked at the harbor that he still wore flip-flops. Sebastian's text had pissed him off. The guy never explained anything when it came to Rumer. He had no clue how Rumer found out, or exactly what she knew, but he didn't have any choice, but to find her, and bring her home.

The sunset cast a beautiful purplish glow to the sky. From the lights of the guitar on top of the Hard Rock Café to the blue neon water waves on buildings, the harbor slowly switched from tourist attraction to local hot spot. He knew exactly where she'd be. She loved the water, especially the boats. She'd been young, too young to remember so well, but she did. Before her mother succumbed to breast cancer, she and her parents had taken a dinner cruise on the harbor. It was one of her last happy memories she had of her "whole" family.

The vibrant yellow of her dress was slightly muted by the moonlight, but she was still beautiful. A breeze wafted across the harbor ruffling the edges of the dress where it lay against her legs. She tucked the fabric of the dress tighter underneath her thighs, and leaned back against the bench.

"Rumer," he said when he was close enough. "Can I join you?"

She didn't even look at him.

He sat on the small metal bench and waited. Nothing.

"How did you know I was here?" she asked.

Who would ever want to admit that another man gave him a heads up to what was happening with his own wife, but in this case there was no way around it. And from the blank expression on her face this conversation wasn't going to be easy. She was locking away everything inside of her, and he couldn't let that happen. "Sebastian texted me."

She turned to him. "What did he tell you?"

"Nothing."

She turned away. "Why are you here?"

"Where else would I be?" He'd never had a hard time talking with Rumer. They'd always been able to share what was on their hearts and minds. "Anything you want to ask, I'll answer."

"I don't believe you."

"No more lies or secrets." No matter how much losing her as a wife would hurt, losing her as a friend would kill him. "I promise."

"Why did you take me there knowing she worked there?"

"I knew she'd be gone for a while," he forced himself to continue, "I didn't expect your program to be so strong."

"What?" she asked as she turned and glared at him.

"No. I mean...I knew it would be good, but I didn't think you'd want to get so involved. Sebastian needed some help, but because you are my wife, I didn't think he'd agree to allow you to stay when he knew Gabriela would return. It was a gamble."

"So, you were betting on Sebastian being a jerk, and loving Gabriela enough to kick me out before she came back to work." She paused. "Why did she tell me she worked at a nail shop?"

He considered that one. "She owns one. Sebastian helped her buy it. Maybe she didn't want you to connect her to the center and Sebastian."

"But, you told me that you'd met her there."

"Yes, but she might have thought you'd try to cause some sort of problems for Sebastian and the center, if you knew she was his sister." Gabriela would protect Sebastian as fiercely as he'd protect her.

Long strangling moments passed without her saying anything. He followed her eyes as they flitted over boats parked at the harbor, or couples walking while holding hands. Somewhere in the distance a saxophone played in rhythm to the waves of the river. The harbor could be incredibly romantic. The last time they'd been there was months ago, date night. They'd arranged everything with his parents, and spent the entire night alone. After dinner, they'd stayed at one of the hotels until morning. The memory of the feel of her in his arms pleased him, but it didn't excite his body like his thoughts of Gabriela which tore him from his sleep drenched in sweat. It'd become too routine for him to get up, strip from his clothes, handle his erection, and go back to sleep.

"You and Sebastian used me in your own twisted game of payback."

He hadn't meant to give Sebastian what he needed to hurt her. And nothing in him had intended to be part of any game of "payback." He'd only meant to save his marriage. To prove to his wife and himself that he was one hundred percent man. Instead, he'd hurt her, lost Gabriela, and wanted so badly to go against everything inside of him, and beat Sebastian senseless.

"No. I never wanted you to become a part of any fight between me and Sebastian." He placed a hand on her thigh. It trembled softly under his hand, and he pulled it away. She didn't want him to touch her. "I thought it would make you understand me better. I hoped it would save our marriage."

The normally soft features of her face were hard and stoic. Her profile hadn't softened at his words, in fact, they'd become even more unreadable.

"You know, you were the only man I'd ever loved." She paused. "I thought we'd love each other forever. We'd have maybe two more children. Thanksgivings would be big and crowded with people as our babies grew, married, and had children of their own." Tears began to fall. "I had dreams of us being old and grey and in love." She finally turned toward him. "Stupid fantasy, huh."

Even if she slapped his hand away, he had to reach out and touch her. He cupped the side of her face with one hand. "I had those same dreams"—he gulped down the knot in his throat—"I never imagined I'd fall out of love with you."

"Then how did it happen?"

"Are you still in love with me?" he asked without fully knowing why. He knew the answer.

She placed one of her hands over his where it held her cheek. "Yes," she hesitated, "but not the way I did when I was twenty." She clutched his hand in hers as she moved it from her face to her lap. "Why did this happen to us?"

"I don't know, but I would never be able to live with myself if I thought you hated me." When she didn't immediately respond, he pushed himself to continue. "Do you hate me?"

Her hand tightened on his. "I did." She shifted to angle her body so that she could face him more. "I wanted everything to be because of you. Another man that disappointed me."

"Rumer—"

"—no, I get it. I know it's not your fault. You are nothing like my father. You didn't just run away, and bury your head in the sand. You didn't seek out Gabriela. Somehow, the two of you found each other, and when you tried to walk away, she tried to stop it."

"I hate that happened." He did. Gabriela never should've gone to her. He should've been the one who told her everything. "I never meant for any of this to happen the way it did."

"I know. But, it did." She released his hand. "I don't want to be in a loveless marriage. I don't want our children to grow up thinking they must accept only part of someone. I want them to know what it means to be loved like we once loved each other."

"I don't want a divorce, but I know you're right." He admitted it to himself at the same time he did her. "I would never want Maddie to be with a man like me. Or, Ty to—"

"—never say that." She rubbed her free hand along one of his arms. "You are one of the best men I know. You tried to make our marriage work, but"—she dropped her hand back to rest with the other one holding his—"we both stopped being 'in love' with each other."

"Are you in love with Sebastian?" he asked, a little too angry. He no longer had the right.

"I don't know." She wiped away tears as they fell on his arm. "I am so hurt and confused by everything that I think I need a break."

"What does that mean?"

"I want to take some time to be alone. I'm going to take the kids and go back to grandma's house and try to figure a few things out."

"Rumer, I love you. I would do anything you ask, if...if we can still be friends. I don't want to be one of those fathers who has to pick up his kids up from a neutral zone because his ex-wife hates him."

"That'll never happen to us," she smiled, weakly.

Luke latched onto that smile. It meant there was hope. He wasn't sure if it would take months or years, but one day, he and Rumer would be friends, again. One day, the pain he'd caused her wouldn't touch her heart the way he knew it did. His betrayal, Gabriela, Sebastian, all of their games and lies would change her, but he would give her the time she needed to become just friends.

Unspoken anger, disappointment, and sadness weaved a thick net of tension through Rumer's meeting room. Eleven sets of eyes were glued to her every movement. The suit she'd chosen to wear restricted her ability to take a deep breath. She loosened the three buttons on the jacket, but even that didn't do enough. She removed the jacket, and twisted in her chair to hang it from the back.

RUMER

When she shifted to focus her attention on the men waiting for her next word, she got the question she knew would come.

"Why?" Kevin asked.

"I'm moving to Hampton, VA with my children." She'd tried to prepare herself, but nothing she'd done would ever have given her the strength she needed to not want to wrap her arms around him, and promise him whatever he asked. She inhaled, and stiffened her back. "Kevin, I wish I could say I know when I'll return." She allowed her eyes to scan everyone, but one. "If there was any other way for me to do what I need to do, I wouldn't leave, but there isn't."

Jake, one of her students who'd graduated, but had problems with people at work spoke, "Ms. Rumer, we all hate to be selfish, but you're the best group leader we've had." He scanned the room for support, and found it when everyone nodded their heads in agreement. "What happens to us? The group."

This time she had to focus on the one person she wanted to avoid. "Sebastian, will lead the group until he finds someone else he thinks is suitable." She smiled. "You guys are in the best hands possible."

Kevin glanced over his shoulder at a silent Sebastian.

"No offense, man, but Ms. Rumer is the best." He turned to face her again.

Sebastian said, "I agree."

He'd stood in the back of her group the entire time, never saying a word. Did he think he'd intimidate her into staying? That wouldn't work. Nothing would work. It had taken her a few weeks to make up her mind, but she'd known it the day she sat on the harbor with Luke. She needed to spend time with her kids, and regroup. Her heart had been dragging her around by a leash, and she needed to understand what it wanted. Luke and Sebastian pulling on her, each in his own way, would do nothing but confuse her more.

"Thank you all for making this such a wonderful experience for me." She stood and they all stood and surrounded her. Arms wrapped around her, so many that she could barely count. The potency of their combined hugs and words of encouragement strengthened her. Her heart begged her to stay, but her head knew she was doing the right thing. Returning kisses and hugs to everyone, she couldn't help notice there was one who broke away from the circle, and hovered at the doorway before vanishing through it.

Kevin didn't say good bye.

She took the steps with Sebastian on her heels, unlike last time, she wasn't running or crying. Gabriela appeared in front of her at the bottom of the stairs. The anger she'd once had toward her was gone, but still she didn't want to talk to her. She didn't stop walking. The woman glanced over Rumer's head, and before she reached her, she stepped away disappearing back into her office.

With a soft click, Rumer closed the door behind her, and didn't look back.

Chapter Twenty-One

Summer rushed away in Hampton. Shorts and flirty dresses gave way to jeans and jackets for fall. Rumer sat on the porch with grandma Mae watching Maddie roll around in leaves laughing like there was nothing better in the world. The only thing she could think about was what a pain in the butt they were to rake and bag. Tyler giggled as he swatted at brightly colored turtles and snails dangling from his play pen placed between her and grandma Mae.

She refreshed her cup of tea by adding more water from the beautiful red cast iron teapot she brought with her from home. She offered to do the same for her grandmother, but she'd refused proclaiming she had her cup just right, perfect mix of honey and tea.

A little more than a month had passed since she'd seen Luke, or Sebastian. Luke had driven up almost every weekend to see the children, and to ask when she would return. She still wasn't sure. He'd agreed to give her the house, and pay child support as a part of their divorce. It was more than enough for her to be able to take care of the kids, and herself until she could find a job. A job. Not working at the center had been harder than she'd thought, not just because of Sebastian, but she missed the boys. A few had called her, but not Kevin. She had no idea how he was doing, or what. She'd broken down once or twice and texted Sebastian to ask about Kevin.

Pain ached in her knowledge that Sebastian hadn't once reached out to her since she'd been gone. And his text responses had been short and informative, nothing else. No questions about how she and the kids were doing. No questions about when she'd return. A part of her had convinced herself that he cared for her as much she had him. But, sitting on her grandmother's porch sipping tea, reality hit in a big way. If a man like Sebastian wanted her, he never would've allowed her to walk away.

Her phone rang.

"Rumer, you have to come home," Luke began, "something's happened to Kevin."

"What?" The desperation in his voice scared her. "Is he okay?"

"It's pretty bad." He paused. "He and Gabriela are both in the hospital."

Why would they both be in the hospital? "I'll be there in a few hours. Text me the information, and I'll meet you there." Why hadn't Sebastian called her?

She explained everything to grandma Mae, kissed the kids, and told them she'd be back. She packed a bag because she didn't know how many days she'd be gone, and hopped into her car. Hours later, when she parked next to the red sign in the emergency parking lot, she noticed the message on her screen.

We need you. Kevin's hurt.

The message was from Sebastian.

Nurses had threatened to send Sebastian home, if he didn't sit and take a break. With his sister stretched out in one room, and Kevin in another how was he supposed to kick his feet up and sleep? Again, he checked his phone, but still no response. Sitting on the ledge of a window in Kevin's room he rested his head against the frame where it met the glass, and closed his eyes. He couldn't believe she hadn't responded. She might not give a damn about Gabriela, but he never thought she'd ignore Kevin. When Luke arrived to watch over Kevin and Gabriela—the guy came in handy for something—he'd left to take Kevin's grandmother home. He opened his eyes to glance at the kid when he heard him moan. How could anyone leave him alone? No parents showed up. The other boys from Rumer's group had been filing in and out, but no family. Rumer had been all he had except for his grandmother. The kid's boyfriend hadn't even shown his face, and he was the reason for all of it.

He heard the creak of the hospital room door, and he opened his eyes.

Slowly, she removed a jacket, and placed it in a chair near the door, and walked toward Kevin. Dark jeans hugged her hips and thighs. A thin long-sleeved sweater clung to her small breasts and arms. Briefly, she glanced at him before focusing her attention on Kevin. She placed a hand on his forehead sweeping away hair that was much longer and a different color than the last time she saw him. His eyes fluttered trying to open as if he knew she was there. She bent and kissed him on the forehead. Sebastian fought the desire to reach over wrap his arm around her waist and pull her to him. She stood, but still the curve of her butt enticed him. His hands ached to grip and caress her bottom making him familiar in a way no other man would ever know, if he ever got the chance, just once.

She turned and closed the gap between them. "I'm sorry. I didn't see your text till I parked outside."

That explains that one.

"What happened?" she asked. A tear dangled from the tip of an eyelash.

He reached up, and swiped the tear away with a thumb. The softness of her skin pierced a hole in a damn of emotions he wasn't sure he was ready to handle, or to have rejected. Allowing his hand to slide down her arm, and then rest on the tempting curve of her hip, he spoke, "His boyfriend's brother and a group of his friends waited for him outside of the center."

Her right hand went to her chest. Splayed across her heart, her tears fell.

"Gabriela heard the fight, and went outside to help. Everyone else, including me was gone."

He shifted his body allowing space for her between his legs, and she tucked herself between his them, and rested her forehead on his chest. He tugged at the ponytail that hung from the back of her head. "Hey, they're both okay.

139

RUMER

Remember, I taught Gabby how to fight, and she never goes into a fight empty handed. She called the police before she jumped in. She and Kevin held their own."

She pulled away and, after wiping at her flood of tears with the back of one hand, she went to Kevin's side. "He's so bruised. His eyes are swollen shut," she whispered. "I thought you had security patrolling."

"I do, but they were on break." He tried to control his anger. "The bastards must've been watching. They knew it was only the two of them in the building." He smiled at his next thought. "I don't think they expected Gabby to be so strong."

She smiled. "I guess you were right to teach her. Maybe you should teach me, too."

"No, I don't want you to fight."

She folded her arms across her body. "You want to treat me like a child."

"No," he responded. He didn't. He just didn't want to be responsible for crushing anyone who thought it would be okay to fight with her. "I want you to be able to protect yourself, but you don't have to fight. Not like me. Or, Gabby." He nodded at Kevin. "Or, him."

"How is Gabby? I came straight to Kevin's room."

"She's okay." He raked a hand through his hair. "I was worried because there were four of them, and she only had her surgery a few months ago."

"Oh, I forgot about her surgery..." her voice trailed off. "Maybe I should go and say thank you for protecting Kevin."

"Luke's with her." He didn't want her to be surprised when she walked into the room down the hall to find her husband. As soon as he'd called him, the guy had asked for all the details, and hadn't left Gabby's side since he'd arrived. "She's right down the hall."

He watched as she glanced at the door and them him. "Should I go, now? Is she conscious?"

"I think...I think she's doing better now." As soon as Luke had entered the room, his sister's disposition changed.

Even with one swollen eye, she smiled and held out a hand for him. The guy kissed her cracked bruised knuckles, and promised to be there until she kicked him out.

"I'll be back."

He didn't want to see her leave, but he had to give her time to make peace with the love the two people down the hall shared. When he knew she'd finally allowed her heart to heal, and she was ready to love him, he wouldn't let her run away again.

Rumer dragged herself down the hallway, slowly. Time had passed, true, but was it enough to prepare herself to see the man she'd dreamed of loving forever embraced by someone else. What if she walked in and they were kissing? The thought of her Luke with someone else made her a little jealous. She no longer had a claim on him or his heart. But, he'd already moved on from his love for her, while she struggled with allowing herself to care for another. The moment she'd walked into Kevin's room, and mentally chastised herself for wanting to throw herself into Sebastian's arms, she knew the truth of her heart.

When she reached Gabriela's room, she stopped, and took a second to prepare herself.

Walking through the door, tears stung her eyes at the sight of the smile Luke wore unbidden at her entrance. Gabriela's mouth upturned in its own invitation to join them. Luke stood and raced toward her scooping her into a bear hug of an embrace. She threw her arms around him because she'd missed him. When he felt her return his hug, he squeezed her tighter. Kissing her squarely on the lips, and then he placed her feet back on the ground.

"I'm so glad you came." He paused. "Did you bring the kids?"

"No, I'm sorry, I was so concerned. I left them with grandma, and jumped on the road."

His smile faded a little. "This is probably no place for them anyway, but"—he kissed her on the cheek—"I'm glad you're here."

"Me, too," Gabriela said, softly.

She stepped around Luke and approached Gabriela's bedside. "I'm sorry this happened to you." She reached for one of Gabriela's hands, and squeezed. "But, thank you for taking care of him when I wasn't here."

Gabriela smiled, and Rumer accepted the woman's gesture of kindness. Deep inside of her, the anger she'd been nursing began to crack and fall away. Gabriela understood Kevin's pain in a way she never would. There would never have been the question of if she'd help him. Gabriela would always have tried to protect any of the kids in the program, regardless of the consequences to her own safety. The physical strength and power of the woman lying battered in the bed in front of her had never been in question. But, she had wondered how cold her heart had to be to break up a family and cause her so much pain. But, as she watched Luke and Gabriela, silently, reassure each other, and as she accepted that Gabriela had been the one there to protect Kevin, she admonished herself for being the coward who ran.

She leaned over and kissed Gabriela on the cheek. "Take care of him," she whispered. The crooked smile that spread across bruised bronze skin confirmed that Gabriela understood she didn't mean Kevin.

After a few minutes of discussing the children, she left the two of them alone, and returned to where she'd left Sebastian at Kevin's bedside.

Chapter Twenty-Two

A twenty minute conversation wouldn't erase all the pain between Gabriela, Luke, and Rumer, but she couldn't help but feel better about what the future might hold for all of them. As she neared Kevin's rooms Sebastian's voice burst through the closed door at her. He was angry, and if she didn't get to him, she wasn't sure what would happen. She picked up her pace, but didn't want to flat out run. Whoever was on the other side of the door was about to be pummeled, and she wondered if they knew that.

Waving away nurses and doctors as they paused and glanced over at the room, she smiled and nodded to reassure them she'd take care of whatever was happening on the other side of the door. She was more than certain they had more important things to do, so she didn't expect any of them to question her, and they didn't.

Pushing the door open only enough to allow her body to slide through, she quickly shut it behind her.

Sebastian stood facing down a much smaller younger man. The kid's jeans were torn, and one of his eyes was swollen, but the punches hadn't been thrown by Sebastian. Someone definitely would've heard a fight. And no matter how much Sebastian blocked the boy's attempts to get to Kevin, he kept trying. She was confident the young man would've fought Sebastian—hard, even if it meant another black eye.

"Gary," she said, softly.

Neither of the men responded.

"Gary." She forced herself to wedge her body between the two men. "Take a seat." She pointed at a vacant chair.

He glared at her as if he wouldn't obey, but then something inside of him decided not to fight her, too, and he sat.

Taking Sebastian's wrist, he allowed her to pull him to another corner of the room after a few tugs.

"Sebastian, this is Kevin's boyfriend."

"I know." He glanced over her head at the kid who'd angled his chair so that he could keep an eye on Kevin. "Why do you think I was trying to throw him out?"

"Look at him Sebastian"—she pointed at Gary—"he has a black eye, too. His clothes are all torn. He was fighting somebody." She paused. "Remember when we told Kevin that Gary's brother might hurt him, too. Well...doesn't it look like something happened." She knew her next words would curb Sebastian's desire to rip out the young guy's arms. Placing a hand on his arm, she said, "I think he needs your help as much as Kevin."

She knew exactly when her words set in with him. He kissed her on the forehead, and walked over to Gary.

The young boy's body tensed, but he didn't run. He waited to see what Sebastian's next move would be.

"She thinks"—he glanced over his shoulder and clasped his hands behind his back—"your brother made your face look like that. True?"

"Yeah."

"Why?"

"Because I wouldn't tell him where Kevin was staying." He glanced at Kevin when he heard a moan. "He and his friends beat me, and then they said they'd just go to the center and wait for him. I tried to call him, but"—he used the bottom of his torn t-shirt to wipe away tears—"he's been acting different since...since Ms. Rumer left. I hoped he wouldn't be there."

Sebastian glanced back at her, but stood where he was. She wanted to go slink into a dark hole. But, that's what caused the problem in the first place. Kevin and every young man in her group had needed her, but she'd turned her back on everyone. Left them all without anyone for them to confide in. She walked over to Kevin's bed, and sat on the space next to his thigh. She prayed he'd be okay because when he opened his eyes, she wanted him to know that she'd never leave him again.

His story was like so many other kids in her group. His parents didn't accept him. So, they left him to fend for himself. The part of their story that was the same was that his mother's mother had cared for him when no one else would, just like hers. Hot and heavy her tears began to fall. The thin blanket covering his small body stuck to his skin where her tears moistened it.

"I'm sorry, Kevin. Please forgive me," she said.

Sebastian and Gary both flanked her. Sebastian's big rough hand wrapped around her neck, and she relaxed her body into it. He stepped in closer, and she could feel the hard muscle of his stomach and thigh. She rested her back against him, and didn't feel ashamed to cry in front of him and Gary over the battered body of one of the bravest men she knew.

"Ms. Rumer, this isn't your fault," Gary said. "I should've stood up to my brother a long time ago. I let him intimidate both me and Kevin because I was afraid."

"No, Gary, this isn't on you," Sebastian said. "Your brother and his friends are afraid of something they don't understand. Family should stick together." He placed a free hand on Gary's shoulder. "They never should've attacked you or Kevin. If you need me to speak with your parents or anyone, I can."

"No, I took care of everything." Gary touched the tips of his fingers on one hand to his busted bottom lip. "My parents didn't need much more to convince them when they saw me. They waited with me for my brother to come home. When they threatened him, he told them everything, and gave his friends up quick." He smiled.

He glanced at Kevin again, and Rumer stood to let him take her place at his side, and hold his hand, even if she didn't want to let go. He should be by Kevin's side.

"They turned him in. It broke my mom's heart. She was still crying when I left. But, because they turned themselves in, the lawyer my parents got him thinks everything will be okay. My parents didn't want him to think attacking me or Kevin was okay."

"You should be so proud of your parents," Sebastian began, "some parents never come around like yours."

"I know, but it may be too little too late. Kevin may never forgive me when he wakes up."

Rumer smiled. "I don't think that's true. If you ask me, seeing you will be the best possible thing that could happen."

"You think so?" he asked.

"Positive." She knew how much Kevin loved him. If he wasn't there when he woke, he'd suck it up like he did everything, but having him there would erase all other pain. She gave herself permission to snuggle a little closer to Sebastian, and he wrapped his arm tighter around her shoulders pulling her nearer. She didn't want to read too much into it because he was the kind of guy that would give anyone who needed comfort support, but she loved the way she fit against him. If she never had the chance to feel it again, she'd remember every hard toned muscle.

"Gary, we're going to step outside. Can you watch him for us for a while?" Sebastian asked.

"Got it," he said.

Sebastian grabbed her hand, and dragged her down the hall to the elevator. Within moments, they were outside standing underneath the awning indicating the entrance to the emergency room. She wrapped her arms around her body, and rubbed her hands up and down her arms because it was a lot cooler than when she'd arrived.

Sebastian removed the lightweight jacket he'd been wearing, and draped it around her shoulders. If she were naked, she could've worn the thing as a dress. It swallowed her, which he didn't like because he loved her curves and was happy to see she'd stopped hiding them behind sweats and dresses that didn't highlight them.

He maneuvered her into a darker corner off to the side of the entrance because the constant flow of people in and out of the emergency room entrance affected his concentration.

"Are you staying?" he asked.

"I have to go back for grandma and the kids, but then I'll be back."

"What does that mean?"

"We've filed for divorce, but we both want to have a really good friendship because of the kids."

Yes, they would have to be friends because of their children. Where would she work? But, mainly where would her almost ex-husband live. He knew from personal experience how easy it was to take advantage of a situation, and accidentally find yourself in bed with someone.

"Where will Luke live? With you and the kids until it's final?"

"No"—she wrapped herself tighter in his jacket—"he found an apartment."

He stepped a little closer, and she didn't try to run. Placing one hand, palm out, on the wall, he let the other slide up and down her arm. "Do you still love him? Do you still hate my sister and me?"

That's what he really wanted to know. Did she hate him? He could deal with a lot of things, but not with her hating him, even if he did deserve it.

Her eyes glanced down before meeting his again. "I don't hate you...not anymore."

Honest.

"I did for a second. You and Luke used me in your own stupid games. Even Gabriela tried. It wasn't fair for all of you to know what was going on, but I didn't. I thought I was trying to save my marriage, but that wasn't the truth and you and Luke knew it."

Pushing off the wall, he tried to step back, but she placed a hand on his side stopping him. Instantly, his mind wandered, and he imagined her beneath him with both hands on him holding him in place as he drove deep inside of her. He tried to push back again, but not because he wanted to. He needed to step away before she noticed the erection pushing at the zipper of his jeans.

"Sebastian," she said.

She'd taken his moving away as anger, but it wasn't. He nudged her into an even darker corner hoping she wouldn't notice why, and returned to his earlier stance. This time, he allowed the fingers of his free hand to caress the soft curve of her cheek. His hand traveled down the soft cotton of the sweater to her neck, and he suddenly hated fall.

"What about me?" he asked.

"What..."

He leaned in closer, and touched his lips to her cheek.

"Are you ready for me, now?"

He dropped his free arm to her waist, and pulled her tight against his body. He let her feel for herself what his words meant. She sucked in a quick short breath, and then released it. Warm breath blew against the thin cotton of his shirt.

"Sebastian," the male voice said.

It wasn't Rumer's moan of his name that he heard, but another familiar, but unexpected voice. Reluctantly, he pulled away, but his squeeze of Rumer's hip kept her right where he wanted her. He dropped his arm from the wall, and angled his body, slightly.

"Dad. Mom." He thought maybe his mom might show, but he never expected his dad. "I wasn't expecting you."

"Sorry, it took us so long. You know I never check the voicemail on the phone at the house," his mother said. "Is she okay?"

No one would ever know his mother was sixty-five, if she didn't tell them. But, tonight, the deep lines in her forehead, and the dark circles under her eyes gave away every year. Even his father's normally perfectly groomed hair was disheveled and his clothes were slightly more wrinkled than he knew his dad would normally allow.

"Gabby will be happy to see both of you."

Rumer squirmed a little against him.

"Hi, I'm Rumer Wilson." She stepped out of his grasp, and extended a hand to both of his parents. Stripping his coat from her shoulders, she pressed it against his stomach where it fell perfectly to cover his aching arousal which had been much happier pressed against the soft warmth of her body. "Sebastian, you show them Gabriela's room, and I'll go check on Kevin."

Before he could say anything, she disappeared back into the hospital leaving him with his parents. He and his mom and dad had some things to discuss, but her quick getaway had more to do with the two of them than his parents. It wouldn't matter because she'd already said she was back to stay, and Luke was moving into an apartment. He had plenty of time to catch her, and he would.

Chapter Twenty-Three

Sebastian's parents didn't say much of anything on the elevator ride up to Gabriela's room. For all their faults, he gave them respect for leaving the past behind, and coming to his sister's bedside when she needed them. They'd cared for her while she healed from her surgery, and now, they raced to her bedside after she'd been attacked outside the center. Something inside of him was just as angry at the bullies turning themselves in as happy. His blood boiled with desire to knock the hell out of the men that had the balls to come to his center and attack one of his kids and his sister. But, they weren't men. They were kids. Stupid, ignorant almost men. They needed to be taught, not beat. Rumer understood that, and she was teaching him.

Rumer thought she understood him, but she had no real idea about his childhood. She'd chosen a man like Luke for her husband. If she really knew all of the brutal details of his youth, would she be able to love him.

Gabriela had been the only person who could calm him down when he was younger, and then she'd left. Just weeks ago, his sweet sister tried to leave again because of him. She didn't want him to turn back into the man he'd been when they were children.

"Sebastian, are you okay?" his mother asked. "You...you haven't seen the people who did this...have you?"

Apparently, his mother and father hadn't forgotten the man he used to be either.

"They're in police custody." The elevator dinged, and he held the door open for them to exit. He walked out behind them, and led them to Gabby's room.

His parents stopped at the door. "Son, let the police handle this one," his father said.

"I will as long as they handle it the right way." He'd stay out of it if the police threw the bastards in jail, and left them there for a few years. If not, he'd consider their ages while he taught them the lesson they wanted to teach his sister. He motioned for them to enter the room.

Luke and Gabriela both seemed startled by their visitors. He was sure for different reasons, but their expressions mirrored as his parents took a position on the opposite side of Gabby's bed from where Luke sat.

In true "old school" style, Luke stood and introduced himself to their parents, and offered their mom his seat. He didn't think he'd ever meet Rumer's dad, but her grandmother meant the world to her. If the woman didn't like him, he'd probably never get another chance. Studying Luke might teach him something. The "perfect gentleman" could give him a few pointers.

"I can't believe you came." Gabby's tear fell fast.

It'd been a long long time since he'd seen her cry. He'd be willing to bet that even when the college kids circled her and Kevin, she didn't cry. A picture of her kicking off her ridiculously high heels bracing herself as he'd taught her and readying her punch flashed in his head. His sister had always been strong, but here with everyone in the room who loved her by her side, for once, she let herself be vulnerable.

"Dad," she tried to speak through her tears, "I thought you...you wouldn't care."

The words were a verbal punch. His father's body actually seemed to sway from the weight of it. Then, his father surprised him.

"Why wouldn't I? You're my daughter, too."

"But—"

"—no. No more of the past." He wrapped his arm around his wife, their mother, and tucked her to his side, and then he grabbed Gabby's hand. "We're family." He glanced over his shoulder to where Sebastian stood against a wall watching. "Family sticks together. It may have taken me some time to figure it out. But, I hope you'll give me the chance to be the father I should've been."

Gabby's smile was the only response he received because she cried too hard to speak.

Luke kissed Gabby on the cheek. "I'm going to go and check on Kevin."

Sebastian knew it was his way of giving the family privacy to get rid of some old ghosts. When Luke walked by him, he said, "Tell Rumer I'll catch her later." The guy glared at him for a second, before he cleaned it up, and nodded at him as he left the room.

It was clear to anyone in the room who Luke was in love with, but Sebastian didn't have a doubt in his mind that he still loved Rumer and, suit and tie aside, he was certain the man would try his best to knock him out, if he thought he'd hurt Rumer in any way. The feeling was mutual, if he hurt Gabby.

Days after she'd been admitted, Luke wheeled Gabby out of the hospital. The magic of make-up hid the few bruises that marred her skin. He replayed the past months through his mind as he walked. Finally, things seemed like they just might work out. No one had threatened to kick him or Rumer out of their circle of friends because of their divorce.

He locked the wheels of the chair in place at the car, and opened the door. Bending to scoop Gabby from the wheelchair, she stopped him.

"I can walk," she laughed.

"Sorry," he responded.

She leaned and kissed him. He wanted to pull her into him, and take his time exploring every inch of her. But, the sunlit parking lot of the hospital definitely wasn't the place for what he wanted. He'd waited for a long time. He could hold out a little longer.

"Luke." A woman's voice.

He turned to find himself staring into the face of one of the nosiest people he knew. Tamika Houser.

"Hi Tamika."

Gabby pushed at the car door attempting to stand, but he wouldn't allow it. Turning away from Tamika, he shoved gently on Gabby's hip, and she conceded as she slid into her seat. Focusing his attention back on his church member, he spoke, "What are you doing here?"

"Visiting some of the patients to hand out toys and read to some of the children with other members of the committee. What about you?"

He walked to the end of the car in an effort to circle to the driver's side and leave. He didn't feel like being under this woman's microscope. Part of him was sure he wouldn't pass the test.

"Picking up a friend who needed a ride."

"Oh." She glanced at the passenger in his car. "I'm sorry to hear about you and Rumer. If you ever need to talk or want to meet for coffee, I hope you'll call me." She smiled.

"Sure Tamika." He made it to his side of the car, and opened his door. "Right now, I have a lot on my plate, but when things die down, maybe." He waved good bye. "I'll talk with you later."

For almost as long as they'd been married, Rumer had warned him about Tamika. According to her, the woman made every effort to be near or around him waiting for any opportunity was the way Rumer put it.

Starting the engine, he turned toward Gabriela. "I'm sorry about that."

"What? Her? Or, you?"

What had he done? Put her in the car, and dismissed a woman who had chased after him for years. "What's that supposed to mean?"

"You didn't want her to meet me." She stared out of the window on her side of the car. "I thought you said you could handle this."

"I wasn't trying to hide you." He didn't think so. "That woman is the biggest gossip I know."

"So, what?" She shifted in her seat, placing as much distance between them as possible. "It's because you're trying to keep me a secret." She sat, silently. "Would you have done the same thing if I was Rumer?"

He mulled over her question as he backed the car out, and headed toward her apartment. "I wasn't trying to hide you. I just didn't feel like having a conversation with Tamika." He didn't answer the rest of her question because he wasn't sure. Rumer cared less for Tamika than he did. But, he wouldn't have to shove her into the car because they knew each other. That was the only reason, he tried to convince himself.

His words didn't do anything to change her demeanor. If she could've curled up in a ball in the passenger seat, he thought she would've. Reaching for her hand, he paused and put it back on the steering wheel when she looked at him like he was a stranger she might hit.

What should he have done? He was divorcing one woman. Falling in love with another, while trying to avoid one he'd been dodging for years. Silly him thinking everything would be smooth and easy.

Chapter Twenty-Four

Rumer hung up the phone in her new office, content. Grandma and the kids were back, which was great, but she couldn't shake the guilty feeling she had when she left the kids at home. And at least one of the people she trusted most in the world was with her children every day. She'd thought Maddie would miss her, too, but the almost four-year old seemed to be enjoying herself with grandma a little too much, she thought in her most mockingly jealous voice. An image of the perfect moms in her church popped into her head. Sooner or later, they wouldn't be able to hold their tongues about her divorce. There was one church member in particular she knew would be more than happy to hear the news.

Who cares!

She glanced around the small room again, and smiled. Her office! Sebastian had told her of the donations, but she still couldn't believe he had enough to pay her a decent salary for a couple of years. What happened after that they'd decide later? But, for now, she was officially a working single mom.

The young men of her group, including Kevin and his boyfriend, helped her paint it. She didn't know why she chose purple, but the color calmed her every time she walked into the room. The furnishings matched the old wood and metal of the furniture in Sebastian's office.

"Hey," Sebastian's voice.

Sure she'd seen him practically every day for months, but since that night at the hospital things were different.

He closed the door, and walked over to where she sat behind her desk. "Do you have any plans tonight after work?"

Leaning his butt against her desk, he peered down at her waiting for a response. It was hard for her to think when he stood so close. Her skin hummed with a request for his caress, just like that night at the hospital. She'd craved his touch so intensely that the feel of his hand on her hip holding her against him shot desire through her body that immediately pooled between her legs. In an effort to squelch her body's reaction to the memory, she crossed her legs at her ankles and tugged at the bottom of the blue blouse she wore pulling it away from her skin. The cool air from the air conditioning brushed across her skin, and she was thankful. Still her eyes, for a quick moment, lingered just below the belt looped through his jeans. When she focused on his eyes, the grin on his face told her he knew exactly what she'd been thinking.

She cleared her throat. "I was going to cook dinner for the kids and grandma."

"Dinner, huh?" He twisted her chair, and pulled her from her seat. "When do I get an invitation?"

"I...I didn't think you'd want to do something like dinner at my house with my kids." She and Luke had explained everything to Maddie, and she'd cried because her daddy wouldn't sleep in the same bed with mommy, but when they told her he'd be close by and she could still see him every day, she'd smiled and accepted that they'd still be family. But, what kind of first date would dinner at home be? She'd purchased a pink dress which she thought would be perfect for a night with Sebastian. It fit her body in a way no other dress she owned did. There would be no way to slip in wearing that dress while they sat around her dinner table.

Shifting their position, he placed her butt against the desk, and leaned his body against hers. Through the fabric of her dress pants, she could feel the bulge of the desire he held back. Pulling her bottom away from the desk supporting her, she placed her hands on the side of his torso, and pushed her body into his. Placing his hands, palm down, on the desk, he bracketed her between his arms.

Leaning down, he brushed his lips across her ear, and said, "Do that again."

And she did.

This time, he brushed his lips across hers, and she squeezed her hands against the muscle of his sides, and he understood her needy request. Too many nights her dreams had been filled with imaginary kisses and caresses from Sebastian. Refusing to miss this opportunity to finally know his kiss, she stretched up on her tip-toes and balanced herself by holding onto him. Angling her head, she kissed him. Removing one hand from his side, she placed it on his chest, and tugging on the cotton of his t-shirt, she pulled him down into her kiss.

Enjoying the freedom he gave her to explore his mouth, she took her time. A soft nibble of his bottom lip, then kiss of his top one. Then, she used her tongue to trace the seam between his lips begging him to open his mouth. He didn't. Instead, he pulled away, and stared down at her. Without saying anything, he pushed his body into hers. Her butt fell to the desk behind her, and he stepped between her legs. With one hand cupping the side of her face, he kissed her. She opened her mouth, and his tongue tangled with hers. Every nip of his teeth and touch of his tongue increased the need growing inside of her.

She tightened her hold on him, and gave herself over, completely.

She ignored the knock on her office door. But, the person on the other side wouldn't go away. Sebastian lifted his head. She tried to pull him back to her. He smiled and stepped away adjusting the bulge in his jeans in an attempt to make it less noticeable. She didn't think that would be possible. But, she watched with interest that made her want to replace his hands with her own, and move at a much slower pace. She bit the right corner of her bottom lip at the thought.

"If that was your way to take my mind off dinner, it almost worked." He walked to the door to answer it.

"Wait, you're leaving?" Nothing inside of her wanted that.

He stopped before he reached the door. "You're inviting me to dinner?"

"If you want, but you might be bored." She wasn't sure how he'd handle two kids and her grandmother.

He walked back toward her. "You afraid to let me meet your family?"

She rounded the desk and stood in front of him. "No. I just thought our first date would be the two of us." And her grandmother would drill him with questions, not the ideal.

"So"—he leaned down and kissed her—"you want me all alone." He smiled. "We'll discuss dinner later and we'll finish this."

She would like to have some time with him alone, but...finish it!

"Okay." It was the only thing she could get out before he stepped away, and opened the door.

Luke stood on the other side. The drawn expression on his face dampened some of the ache just south of her stomach that wanted her to close the door, and pleasure herself with one more wet and warm kiss before Sebastian left. The guys exchanged glances. One left as the other entered. No bromance there, but at least they didn't growl either.

Luke dropped into the other chair in the room, and everything about him was so familiar: the spread of his legs and the slump of his shoulders. She shut the door on what she was feeling for Sebastian, and put all her attention on her friend. Walking to where he sat, she took her stance behind him and, like she'd done so many times before, she placed her hands on his shoulders with fingers splayed, and began to massage. His head rolled on his neck as she worked the recognizable knots and tension from his shoulders and back. Only when she felt his body relax beneath her fingers did she lessen the pressure associated with each touch.

He leaned his back against the chair, and stretched his legs out in front of him. With his right hand, he reached across his body, and placed it on top of her left one. She paused and looked down into his eyes. Dark black eyes, filled with pain, stared up at her.

She leaned her head down to his, and touched her forehead to the top of his.

There was another knock on the door. Sebastian walked in.

"Rumer"—he stopped at the entrance—"I didn't mean to interrupt."

Rumer lifted her head, and began to try to speak, but—

"It looks like you two were in the middle of something important." He scanned both of them. "Don't worry about dinner. I have something I have to do."

Every touch of his eyes on their body felt like a tiny pin prick in her gut. When he walked out of the room, and closed the door behind him, she wanted to burst through it and stop him. But, he needed to trust her. Luke was the father of her children. Her friend. And she didn't' know if she could ever choose between the two of them. And even though she knew Sebastian wanted her, Luke, she glanced back into his eyes, he needed her.

"If you need to go, I'll understand." He released the hand he still had locked beneath his own. "I can wait."

"No." She looked at the door one more time. It would be okay. She needed it to be, but the tangle of flutters—not the good kind—in her belly was killing her. "I'll find him after we talk." She retrieved her own chair from behind her desk, and seated herself in front of him where she wouldn't miss anything, including the door opening again. And, if it did, he'd know they were just talking, like friends—not lovers.

At the moment, she had no lover. She wasn't sure about Luke, but she didn't think men could wait as long as women. Maybe that's the other reason Sebastian was pissed. Maybe he was tired of waiting on her: to separate, to file for divorce, to move out, to choose him. She forced herself to focus.

"Tell me what's wrong," she said.

"Tamika Houser." He stared at the purple wall behind her. "Last week, she saw me leaving the hospital with Gabby. And from what I've been hearing, she's already busy gossiping at church and some of them work with me. It's spilling over to my job, too."

"What's spreading?" she asked.

"Tamika's telling people I left you for someone at the center."

How did she know so much so quickly? "What? How?"

"I'm not quite sure. Apparently because of the work she does at the hospital, she asked a few questions of nurses, and that was enough for her to piece things together."

"Has she been here and we didn't know it?"

"I don't think so. Somebody would've noticed her."

He was right. She didn't think anyone would miss the statuesque woman with her knee-length business suits. Most of the people, except Gabby and her, wore sweats or jeans, everyday.

"What aren't you telling me?"

"When she saw me with Gabby at the hospital, I guess I didn't handle it right." He slid a hand over his bald head. "Gabby's barely spoken to me in a week. And with all this crap at work, I don't know what to do. How to handle it. I'm doing everything wrong."

She reached for the hand resting on his lap, and sandwiched it between her own hands. "Luke all of this is new to you...and to me. We're going to make mistakes and, hopefully, we'll be forgiven. You and Gabby have been through a lot and, if she's going to be with you, she'll have to get used to you putting your foot in your mouth." She smiled. "You do it so well."

"Hey. Are you kicking a man when he's down?" A slight hint of a smile curved his lips. He glanced at the door. "I didn't mean to cause any trouble between you and Sebastian."

"Don't worry. We have to decide what to do about Tamika." She scrunched up her nose, and he rubbed an index finger along the bridge. "She's nosey. And she's always had a thing for you."

"Now, I think she's just pissed that I didn't choose her after you."

"Humph, I think we should just tell her it will never ever happen not even if she was the last woman on earth."

He raised an eyebrow. "Last woman...well, wait—"

She punched him in the arm cutting off his words.

"Don't even try it." She'd missed the way she and Luke could easily talk with each other. She threw her arms around his neck. "I'm glad we're still friends."

He wrapped his arms around her. "I'll always be here. Anytime you need me to beat Sebastian into submission, you let me know."

"No, never because then Gabby would jump in and then me." She laughed as she sat back in her chair. "It would get ugly, fast."

The mention of Gabby's name sobered him, a little. "What am I going to do? How do I make her forgive me, and keep Tamika out of my business and away from my job? I mean, what does she think...that I'll split from Gabby and get with her to save my reputation?"

"I don't know. She just might think it'll work, and then she can help redeem your reputation in front of everyone."

Deep inside, she wanted to be wrong, but she didn't think she was and, from the look in Luke's eyes, she knew he believed it, too. When he first realized he'd fallen in love with Gabby, he'd thought something similar. That's why he tried to ignore his feelings, and try to throw every ounce of his energy into his family and marriage. She'd agreed to the plan, and it failed. They both were hurt and so were the people that cared for them.

If Tamika couldn't have him for herself, then she'd rather see his reputation destroyed and watch him go down in flames. And because they were divorcing, it wouldn't affect Rumer. It would only lend more speculation as to why, in everyone else's eyes, things were moving so fast because they'd kept a secret for so long. But, for the four people that mattered, dealing with the emotional tsunami around them had been difficult. It'd taken months for the two of them to be able to simply sit in a room and be okay with the fact that they each loved someone else. Now, they had two other people who needed to understand the new love they had for each other, and, for Luke, people wanted an explanation of his love.

And he had to decide if he gave them one, or if he lived and loved who he wanted.

Chapter Twenty-Five

Tamika Houser and her committee of "let's shake down Luke" strolled into the center just after Rumer's group ended for the night. Only Sebastian, Gabriela, and she were still in the building. She didn't know what they were doing because neither had said much to her over the past days, but she like an idiot she waited on Sebastian to come find her. To talk to her. But, she couldn't sit around forever she had to get home to help her grandma prepare dinner.

The three floors would never replace the gym, but she loved the way Sebastian stared at her every time she used them, so she walked them a million times a day, every day. While he made her wait, she might as well have some fun, and show off her "baby fat all gone" body!

As her feet touched the landing on the first floor, she found herself face-to-face with the woman that had, in the course of a couple of weeks, stolen Luke's privacy, and given her a reason to dislike her like no other woman, maybe even more than Gabriela on the day when she first approached her in that grocery store parking lot.

"Tamika what are you doing here." Her voice was too pleasant, but Tamika was surrounded by other members of the church she attended with Luke, and she didn't want to let them all know she hated the woman.

"We"—she spread her arms as if she lead a lynch mob of twenty—"thought we'd come and check out your new job and see for ourselves why you and Luke spend so much time here."

"Did you want to volunteer?" Rumer asked.

"Oh"—she shook her head from side to side, the classic sign of no—"we don't think this is the type of place for members of 'our' church." The left side of her mouth lifted slightly before she replaced it with a much more demure purse of her lips. "I remember this place from the news. Some vandals had written such terrible things on the walls, and destroyed everything inside." She glanced around the front entrance. "It looks like you've all done a lot of work around here to clean it up."

Rumer didn't feel like telling Tamika or her mob anything about the center. But, she said, "When Luke's brother committed suicide, he promised himself that he'd never turn his back on anyone in need of his help, if he could do something about it. This center provides jobs, access to health care, counseling, and support to more people than I think he ever thought he'd be able to help in his lifetime." She paused. "Of course we helped repair the building."

Some of the members of Tamika's gang had lowered their eyes when she mentioned Luke's brother's suicide, and when their eyes returned to hers they seemed less hateful.

The click of stilettos and the thud of heavy steel-toed boots told her the other two people in the building were coming down the stairs behind her. Luke and Gabby hadn't worked out all their problems, but now Gabby would find out first hand who Luke tried to avoid and why. And Sebastian would see why Luke needed not only her support, but theirs.

Gabby stood to her right and Sebastian to her left. He placed his hand at the small of her back, and even though she was dwarfed by the giants beside her, his touch energized her.

"Tamika, we're getting ready to close. What do you need?" she asked.

Tamika's gaze locked on Gabby. "You no longer need your wheelchair." She extended a hand. "I'm Tamika Houser."

The four other sets of eyes surrounding Tamika focused on Gabby.

"Gabriela, Tamika heads several different committees at our church," Rumer did the introduction. "Tamika, Gabby manages the staff here at the center. She, recently, risked her life to save one of my kids. Those vandals you mentioned earlier, they came back with friends. The small angry group attacked one of my kids and, later we found out, one of them beat his own brother."

"Oh my God," Yvonne, one of the committee members, exclaimed.

"Yes, if it hadn't been for that young man's bravery, that mob would've never been brought to justice. That's what this center is all about. Helping people, not hurting them," Rumer said.

"Ladies," Sebastian began, "It's been a pleasure to meet you. If you want to return to volunteer, or make a donation, we'd love it. But, it's been a long day, and we need to lock this place up. We wouldn't want any other crazy groups of maniacs coming through getting the wrong ideas." He flashed his most endearing smile.

He moved his hand from her back, and draped it over her shoulder. Some of the members of the committee glanced at each other, and Tamika's smile beamed. She was entirely too happy.

Rumer looped her arm around Gabby's and said, "Look ladies, it's been great catching up, but you all know I've got little ones at home, and these guys"—she let her head sway left to right—"are coming to dinner, so we really should be going."

Tamika's smile disappeared with Rumer's last words. When she first began her flirtations with Luke, she would agree to baby sit for them, or anything that gave her the opportunity to spend time, in Rumer's opinion, getting too familiar with her kids. Luke had thought she was just being nice, but Rumer knew the woman had always wanted her man. She simply tried to do it in a way that would be okay with everyone at their church.

Rumer broke away from Sebastian and Gabby, and led the group of women to the door. "If you have any other questions, just let me know when you see me at church, or call me." She pasted her best smile on her face, and waited for them to file out.

Tamika was the last one. On her way out the door, she glared at Rumer and then Gabby. "You don't get him either."

RUMER

Rumer's smile broadened to the point where her jaws hurt. "But, I had him. You never will."

"We'll see," Tamika said as Rumer closed the door behind her.

Rumer didn't mean to antagonize her, but she'd pissed her off. Showing up at the center for what? And trying to grill Gabby! She deserved every word she'd said, and more. The two people standing at the bottom of the stairs seemed almost as surprised as she was at what she'd done, if their quiet stares were any indication.

"What? She made me mad." She folded her arms across her chest, and rested her butt against the closed door.

Sebastian approached her, and when he reached her, he encircled her in his arms. He leaned his head down to her ear, and whispered, "I like you when you're angry."

She looked up into his eyes and searched for anything to hint that his words were in any way a lie, and that he was still angry, but nothing. The warmth of the emotion in his eyes flowed through his touch, and she really did want him to join her for dinner. Gabby, too. Mainly Sebastian because she didn't want the night to end. She didn't want him to walk through the door and go his way, and she to go hers.

"Well, then prove it."

The look in his eye told her he was thinking something completely different than dinner, but she liked it. She stepped a little closer, and her breasts rubbed against his torso. One of his hands loosened from her waist, and slid to just above the curve of her butt.

"Excuse me, I'm still here." Gabby teased.

"Go away," Sebastian responded.

"You two are blocking my way out." She walked up to stand beside them. "If you two would move, I'd leave."

Rumer's passion-filled fog cleared enough for her to push, a little, at Sebastian. "No, I invited you two to dinner. Aren't you coming?"

"You were serious?" Gabby asked. "I thought you said that to screw with your oh-so-lovely friends."

Part of her had been, but Luke was coming over for dinner, sooner or later, the kids and grandma would need to meet Sebastian and Gabriela. And it would give them the opportunity to tell Luke what happened.

"Yes, I was serious, and since your brother blew me off for dinner the other day, he can make it up to me tonight."

He placed a hand on her hip, and pulled her against his body. "You sure you want me there?"

Placing both palms on his chest, she said, "Yes." Then, she tip-toed, and kissed him, softly. But, she wanted so much more. When his hand tightened on her hip, she lingered just a bit on his bottom lip before she pulled away."So, Gabby, dinner?" she asked.

Gabby glanced at Sebastian. "Sounds good to me."

Grandma would be surprised, but she knew she'd love the company, and Maddie loved everyone. She didn't think Luke would disagree, but she'd text him so he wasn't blindsided. She couldn't wait for them to meet their kids. Screw Tamika Houser. They would make their own rules.

Sebastian watched Rumer and Luke with their daughter and son. What did he know about kids? Nothing. Rumer approached him with Tyler hoisted on her hip. Her small shoeless feet peeked from beneath the floor-length shape-hugging cotton dress. Ty's drowsy eyes tried to focus on him, but instead, he relaxed his head and rested it on Rumer's chest. When she neared, she sat, and he shifted using his small chubby body the baby blocked Sebastian's ability to get as close as he'd like. Placing Ty on Sebastian's lap, Rumer snuggled underneath his arm. His family life had always been simple: mom, dad, and Gabriela. No time or room for much more than that. There were not a whole lot of people who wanted to be a part of a family that wasn't your "traditional" family.

Ty's round face pushed right up to his. Big brown eyes stared with no amusement. The boy glanced down at his mother perched beneath Sebastian's arm, and then back at his father where he sat with Gabby and Madison. When Ty's eyes returned to his, he couldn't help but think that he was being assessed, and he didn't know if he was passing or failing. Small hands patted at his face and played with his hair. After a yawn that made Ty crinkle his nose and close his eyes, he settled down in Sebastian's lap, where Sebastian and Rumer's thighs met, and closed his eyes.

"I think he's ready for bed," Rumer whispered. "I'll put him to sleep and be right back." She cuddled the baby into her arms and shifted to stand, but he stopped her.

"Can I help?" he asked. He didn't know why he'd asked, but he wanted to be with her.

She smiled and leaned over to kiss him. When she tried to pull away, he wrapped a hand around her neck and held her close. He couldn't believe how quickly he was becoming addicted to the feel of her lips and the taste of her mouth. After another kiss, he let her go.

After announcing to the room that they would put Ty to bed, she glanced over her shoulder at him, and then said, "Come on."

He hid the smile he felt deep inside after noticing how Madison disappeared behind Gabby at the mention of putting someone to bed. And Gabby with her most innocent look on her face focused on her nails, instead of the small child hiding behind her. She could try, but there was no way, she'd be able to deny she was having as much fun as he'd had with the kids, Luke, Rumer, and their grandmother. The lady had a million stories about Rumer and Luke. Ten years was a long time. As he watched Rumer place Ty in his crib and kiss him on the forehead, he again understood how strong this woman was. Small, but strong.

He sat in the overstuffed chair placed beside a big window, and kept watching.

When she was satisfied Ty was okay, she turned to him.

She walked toward him, and he had to remind himself that her grandmother, daughter, almost ex-husband, and his sister were in the other room. She sat on his lap, and wiggled, a little, until she found a comfortable position. What was good for her wasn't necessarily good for him. As she draped a leg over the side of the chair, her butt rubbed against the tip of his penis. He strained to curb the need growing inside of him until she did it again.

"Stop, Rumer."

She'd changed into a long floor-length cotton dress that exposed her arms and hugged every curve he loved. When he placed a hand on her thigh to stop her movements, he snatched it back because the feel of the fabric against her body didn't do anything to help him control himself.

She smiled up at him, and did it again. Harder.

He gripped her thigh and squeezed. "I mean it. Stop."

"Shh"—she dragged a finger down the center of his cotton t-shirt—"you don't want to wake Ty. He's ferocious when he doesn't get his sleep."

Using the fingers of her right hand, she alternated her touch between his nipples. Through the fabric of his shirt, he felt her as she drew tiny circles around his excited flesh. Then, she touched her lips against his neck. Her warm tongue licked from his earlobe to his collarbone. With one hand he gripped the soft cushioned arm of the chair and the other ruffled the bottom of her dress searching for a way beneath the soft annoying cotton.

She widened her legs and, again, she rubbed her round bottom against the hard heavy need of his erection.

Sliding his hand along the soft skin of her inner thigh, he used his other hand to gently pull at the hair that now touched her shoulders. Angling her head so he could see her eyes, he hovered his mouth over hers, "You think I won't do this right here? With our family on the other side of that door, and your son in his crib," he panted.

Her response was another wiggle. He didn't try to hide what he wanted. When she pushed into him, he pushed back. And he took her mouth in a kiss that showed her just how much he wanted her. He allowed his hand to settle on the sensitive mound that he knew wanted his touch.

He pulled away from their kiss, and stared into her eyes. She let her head fall back into the hand that supported her neck, and pushed her body up against his hand.

171

Alternating the push of her pelvis from his penis to his hand, her body claimed his.

Sliding the fingers of his hand beneath the lacy fabric of her panties, the soft curls of her hair hardened his body more. One finger, then two, pushed inside the warm sheath of her body. With his thumb, he played with the swollen nub that made him want to drop to his knees and let his tongue play.

She sucked in a deep breath, and dropped her head back. He couldn't resist the long curve of her neck. His tongue licked and his mouth sucked while he dipped one long finger into the wet warmth of her body. Her body tightened around his intrusion. He used his thumb to massage her clitoris and she released her hold on his finger. He added another one, and the rhythm of her body increased.

He lifted his head, and stared at her. Her lips were slightly open as she panted for air. Her nipples were peaked and called for the touch of his tongue, but because of the position of the chair no matter how he shifted their bodies, he'd have to remove his hand from between her legs to get one of her nipples in his mouth. That pissed him off.

Her eyes locked on him, and he knew what she wanted.

Dropping his mouth to hers, he sucked her upper lip into his mouth, and then released it. Then, her bottom. She reached up and clasped the back of his neck with her hand pulling them tighter together. Their kiss deepened, and so did the force of his fingers into her body. Her tongue played with his and when he thought the moment was right, he used the pad of his thumb to put more pressure on her clitoris, and her body pushed against it.

He felt her body tremble on his lap. He locked his grip on her neck, and kissed her harder, rougher. His own need clawed at him to push up her dress, and let her straddle him while he thrust inside of her. But, as her body calmed, he decided to let his kiss and the touch of his hand be her introduction to his need.

He removed his fingers from her body and adjusted her clothes. He rested his hand in her lap as she shifted.

Reaching for his hand, she took it to her mouth. The fingers that had just teased her body to orgasm, she sucked and licked until his body ached at the promise her mouth made. When she finished, she kissed him with a sweetness that was opposite of the caresses her tongue had just made of his fingers.

"Everybody will probably be wondering what took us so long," she said.

"I can tell them you took advantage of me," he said with a lightness he hadn't had in a while.

"You were so so easy." She smiled.

"So, you were just using me for my body?" he asked.

"Yes."

At the door, he stopped her before she opened it. With her back to his chest, and his erection still heavy and hard in his jeans he pressed it against her soft tempting bottom. "Next time—"

"—will there be a next time?" she asked.

She wanted him as much as he wanted her, but they still had some things that needed to be finalized before he took her. Luke may no longer be the man she wanted, but their divorce wasn't final, yet. And she still had his last name. He slid an arm around her waist, and pulled her tighter against him.

Lowering his head, his mouth caressed her ear as he said, "Next time you can wrap your lips around any part of me you want." He paused. "But, not while you still have his name."

She glanced up at him and, quickly, kissed him before opening the door breaking the intimacy of the small bedroom. Lagging behind her, he calmed his body. He didn't want to rejoin the group and announce to everyone how much he wished he had found another room to drag her into, rip off her dress, and fall into the closest bed.

There definitely would be a next time, and he needed it to be soon.

Chapter Twenty-Six

It had taken a couple of months, longer than both Rumer and Luke had predicted, but they were both certain it had been too long for Tamika. Surrounded by members of their church's board, they were grilled about their marriage and Luke's relationship with a man.

Their church wasn't some throwback from the 1800s. She and Luke both knew there would be some disgruntled voices—Tamika—because of their divorce and his new relationship. She'd never imagined they'd be summoned to an inquisition. And there was no mistake about it, absent the fire and pitch forks, they were definitely at an inquisition. Disappointment and sadness clung to her making it increasingly difficult for her to sit and listen to people she'd loved tear apart the love and relationship Luke had with Gabriela.

Because she stood by his side and wouldn't agree to marriage counseling, some of the members held a sadness in their eyes that made her want to scream when they looked at her. She may have once been as pathetic as the sentiment in their eyes suggested, but not any longer. Because of the time she'd spent with Luke at the center and because of Sebastian and Kevin, she'd grown stronger. She didn't need their pity or anyone to protect her from the big bad world.

Everyone on the board tried to avoid eye contact with them. Most of the members seated around the huge round table couldn't tear their eyes away from Gabriela who sat with Sebastian in one corner of the church's conference room. She glanced behind them to where Sebastian sat, and knew why she couldn't take her eyes off him, but she was sure the scowl on his face, jeans and boots, and t-shirt didn't exactly fit in with the well-dressed members of the board. And Gabriela didn't make it any better by looking like she'd just stepped off a runway; it incensed them more.

RUMER

The members of the board didn't miss out on one chance to drill home the fact that she was a he. At every mention of Luke's relationship with Gabriela, they referred to her as a man. You wouldn't know from Gabby's poker face that the words had touched or hurt her at all, but Sebastian didn't bother to hide what he felt or what he thought about the entire proceeding. You could literally read it all over his face. Once she moved to get up and go to him, but someone from the board had asked her to take her seat. And like a trained school girl she did. But, this was for Luke. A part of him still wanted to be a part of the community they'd helped to grow. She hated what this must be doing to him and to Gabriela.

Tamika asked, "Luke, do you think your new lifestyle 'fits' with the family we've created here?"

"What does that mean?" Luke asked. "Nothing about the way I live is different from anyone else."

"You can't believe that." She looked pass them at the two sitting in the back of the room. "You and Rumer are divorcing, and you've chosen to start a relationship with that person"—she gestured toward Gabriela—"sitting back there."

And not her, Rumer thought.

Rumer didn't feel like sitting through any of the nonsense any longer. "Tamika, is Gabriela your problem, or is it the fact that Luke is dating someone that's not you."

Eyes focused on Tamika. "I, like a lot of women here, may have had a crush on Luke. But, I would never dream of being with a married man, or a gay one."

"Gay?" Luke asked. "Is that what you have to tell yourself, Tamika?" Luke stood and pushed his chair back from the table. Looking back at Gabby, he nodded, and she stood. "She's more woman than I think you could ever be. And I don't have time to entertain any of this anymore." He glanced around the table. "I've been afraid of this moment for a long time. I've loved this place and all of you. But, if this is how you treat me and my friends, then it's not a place where I belong."

Rumer pushed back her chair and stood beside him. "I think we should leave."

Members of the panel shifted in their seats and asked them to retake their positions, but it didn't matter any longer to either of them. Sebastian and Gabby met them at the door, and they left. Rumer had thought leaving their home away from home would be difficult. But, they were different now, and if they didn't fit, maybe that was a good thing. She didn't care anymore. If they couldn't see or understand the work of the center, and love the people as much as they did, then that would forever be their loss.

Gabriela sat next to Luke unsure of what her next move should be. This man had just walked away from something he loved for her. No one had ever done anything like that before, no one except Sebastian. She'd known what she was doing when she walked into his life; he hadn't. And after divorce, kids, her angry brother, when he understood his love for her, he stood his ground and didn't let anything or anyone scare him away.

She patted her hands on her thighs, and he understood her request to stretch out and place his legs across her lap. She removed his shoes and ran her hands up and down the length of his legs. As he relaxed, he rested his back against the arm of the couch with his eyes closed.

Causing him pain had never been her intention; she'd only wanted to be able to love him. But, in loving him, she'd hurt him. If it took every day of her life, she promised herself she'd show him how much she loved him. He'd never regret his decision to take a chance on loving her.

Her doctor had told her it could take awhile before her body was ready for sex. The sensation between her thighs was different, but she was familiar with what it meant. She let her hands continue to explore the feel of Luke's toned leg and thigh through the soft fabric of his pants. As she massaged, she noticed a change in the tension of his muscles and in the new, but familiar ache driving her hands. When her hand nudged the thick weight of his erection lying on his thigh, she stopped. Her eyes glanced up to his, and his tense expression told her he was waiting to see what her next move would be.

She wasn't sure. Would it hurt? Was her body ready? The thought hit her, she was a virgin! She didn't know if her body could handle what was hidden behind the zipper of his pants, but she wanted to find out. Her hand moved to his zipper and, before she knew it, she was on her back, and he was on top of her. Kissing her like he needed her in a way deeper than sex. She gave into his kiss and let his hands explore her body as hers did the same. It felt amazing to touch him without any restrictions, and she was greedy; she wanted to touch every inch of him.

Whatever happened next, she would face it with Luke by her side. And she wanted that to be forever.

Sebastian sat in Rumer's bedroom feeling like a high school kid. Her grandmother and children were asleep, but he couldn't shake the feeling that if the bed squeaked her grandma would come into the room with a shotgun. She didn't make it easy to play the good boy role when she walked around in a t-shirt that hugged her body and yoga pants that made him want to pull them off her and have him straddle her.

Instead, he pulled her onto his lap. "No one has ever stood up for my sister like you and Luke did today." He kissed her because he couldn't resist her mouth, and it calmed some of his need to touch her. "It always seems like it was just the two of us against everybody and everything." He kissed her again. "I never thought a woman like you would walk into my world."

"I didn't like any of what they were saying or doing today." She shook her head. "That's not how they used to be. One person's jealousy poisoned everybody."

He didn't want her to be sad. She and Luke had been through a lot and they'd both lost a part of themselves. Luke had been extremely active in that church. Together they'd helped to build it up from the ground. "Do you think Luke would like to be more involved with the center?"

She threw her arms around his neck. "I think he'd love it. We could probably build out a whole program—"

"—okay, okay, we don't have to plan it now." He slid his fingers through the hair at the back of her head. "I have so many other things I'd like to do, and none of them include talking about your 'almost' ex-husband. Even if I do like him more now."

"I know. I'm sorry." She shifted to straddle him. Pushing him back onto the bed, she undid his zipper.

"Baby," he whispered.

She didn't stop.

She stroked the soft hardness of him through the cotton of his underwear. Her fingers traced the outline of the head of his penis, and he sucked in a breath that did nothing to calm his need. She reached inside his briefs and gripped his erection. He leaned back and braced himself on his forearms on the bed watching every move she made. She was beautiful. The fall of her hair around her face framed it perfectly as she focused on pleasing him. She lifted her eyes to his, and licked her lips.

She wouldn't!

Sliding off his body to her knees, she lowered his pants and his boxers. With his penis fully exposed to her touch, she let her fingers and her tongue play. Wrapping her small hand around the base of his erection, she sucked at the tip. He pushed down the bed resting his feet flat on the floor, and slowly began to push at her mouth begging her to take in more of him. She opened her mouth, and he slid the length of shaft into her mouth. So wet, so warm. Placing a hand behind her head, he pulled her head toward him as he pushed his pelvis toward her. He strained to control his need for her. If her mouth felt this good, how would the rest of her feel?

The walls of her house, no matter how thick, wouldn't conceal his moans or hers from her grandmother or her kids, if he lost control, and took her like he wanted.

He pulled out of her mouth, but she caught the tip and wouldn't let go. She sucked him until he gave in, and pushed back into her mouth brushing against the velvety warmth of her tongue. Placing one hand on both sides of her head, he held her in place and let his pelvis do the work. She didn't fight him. The bed squeaked underneath him, and for a moment, he thought he should stop. But, when she felt him slow down his rhythm, she reached up and dragged her short nails along his chest. Then, she slid her mouth down his shaft until her mouth was flush with his body. She worked her mouth in a way that even if he could stop her, he wouldn't. She used her tongue on the bottom of his erection

RUMER

tightening the suction of her mouth around him, and he lost control.

Burying his mouth in the hair at the top of her head, he muffled the moan she ripped from him. When his body stopped convulsing, she pulled her mouth away, and pushed him back to her bed. Stripping away the rest of his clothes, he rested, naked, in her bed. He watched as she removed her own, and curled up beside him. Her body felt perfect tucked into his, but damn if need didn't sear through his body at every point their bodies made contact. This small woman had beaten him. Reduced him to what? Or, had she made him better?

Better, he decided. Definitely, better.

"Should I leave before the kids and your grandma wake?" he asked. He didn't want to leave. He wanted to stay where he was and hold her all night, but he didn't want her to have to explain anything awkward to the kids or her grandma. And her body next to his tempted him, too much. Each encounter with her made it harder to wait for damn divorce to be final.

"No," she lifted her head from his chest to kiss him, and then returned it to rest against his heart. "I don't want you to leave. I miss you when I'm alone."

Every time he'd visited her and went home alone, it angered him. They didn't have to make love, but he wanted her by his side, in his bed. Knowing she wanted the same made him hard all over again. "You sure?" With nothing between them it was hard to hide his growing desire. He reached down to shift around the weight of his erection.

"I told them you might stay the night." She looked up at him and smiled.

"You think I'm that easy?" He couldn't resist kissing her again.

She glanced down, and then up into his eyes. "No, but I hoped."

"I will always take care of your needs. Baby, you know that." He just didn't want to share her in any way with another man. He wanted to be sure she was all his.

"Sebastian, you won't give me all of you." She sat up in bed. "Not really."

180

Her sudden movements bounced her small ample breasts. Each bounce made his mouth water. "Baby, you know everything." He grabbed her hand, and brought it up to his mouth to kiss the back of it. It wasn't enough. "I'm not hiding anything from you."

"No, I love that you talk to me. But, you won't really make love to me." Her eyes roamed his body.

"Baby, I told you I won't share you." He cupped her cheek with one hand. "I'm not with anyone else. I'm just waiting on you."

"On me to what? Be divorced?"

"Yes." He sat up beside her. "You came to me because you were trying to save your marriage. You helped me with the center. You helped Luke with Gabriela. Now, it's our turn. Just the two of us." He kissed her slow and deep. His erection stiffened at the contact with her tongue. He reached beneath the sheets to fist his erection, and take care of it himself, but he stopped and pulled away. "I need to know I'm the only man you want in your heart and your bed."

"Sebastian, you have to know that."

"Baby, when your divorce is final...I promise whatever you want me to do." He kissed her cheek. Sliding a hand through her hair, he angled her head to give him better access to her neck. Using his tongue he traced the line of her neck. When she thrust her breasts up for his pleasure, he took one tight nipple into his mouth, when her moans could no longer be stifled by his warnings, he released it.

The look of disappointment on her face tickled him. He flicked the wet nipple with his tongue, and turned his attention to the other one.

Her moans tensed every nerve in his body. Pushing the weight of his body into hers, he lowered them to the bed. The scent of her body surrounded him. He couldn't resist slipping a finger into the warm sheath of her body. His erection jumped against his thigh at contact with the moistness of her. Releasing her nipple, he kissed his way down her stomach until his mouth reached his fingers. He removed his fingers and replaced them with his tongue. Damn! She was so excited for his touch. He shifted, and placed the back of one of her thighs on his shoulder. The other leg he pushed out slightly making more room for him.

RUMER

As he dipped his tongue inside of her tasting her excitement, he couldn't control his own body's need to be touched. He wrapped a hand around his penis and stroked in rhythm to her body's thrusts. The deeper his tongue explored her the louder she moaned. Damn he wanted to warn her again, but he'd have to remove his mouth, and that would be hard to do with her small hands pressed against the back of his head. He pulled away long enough to take her clit into his mouth, and suck. Her thighs clamped against his shoulders as her pelvis lifted from the bed. The ache in his own body increased. The push from her hands against his head increased and her legs tightened. His body exploded and as pleasure rippled through him he shifted to lay flat on his stomach allowing himself a better angle to capture all of her in his mouth. As he hungrily sucked and licked at her he held on tight to her when he felt her orgasm take over her. Her taste and scent flooded his senses. Better than a glass of cognac. When her body calmed, he pulled away and positioned himself beside her.

Pulling her into his arms, he said, "I promise you won't be sorry we waited." Didn't she know how hard it was for him to say no to her? He didn't think he'd ever told any woman in his life no. But, this one he wanted in a way he'd never wanted anyone else, and she was making it damn hard to keep saying the simple two-letter word.

He rested in the bed, and she curled up against him again resting her head on his chest. "I'll be old and grey by then."

He laughed and kissed the top of her head. "I don't think I could wait that long." So, kick your lawyer in the ass and make him speed things up. With one hand curved around her bottom and her head on his chest, he fell asleep wishing away his hard-on, and hoping he didn't wake up in the same mood because he may not be able to stick to his own plan.

Epilogue

Six months later...

Rumer sat on the cushions Sebastian had thrown on the floor in front of his fireplace. The warm glow of the fire cast shadows around the small living room. No matter how many times she visited, she was still amazed Sebastian had done so much of the work himself. Paint. Floors. Bathrooms. The living room, decorated so male, still had a warm homey feeling to it, and she loved it more each time she came.

Grandma Mae had agreed to babysit, and give them some time alone. She hated feeling like she took advantage of her grandmother, but she wanted to share her good news with Sebastian when they were by themselves, for so many reasons. One in particular. She'd read the text from her lawyer enough that she had it memorized, but still she couldn't believe it. Adding in the time she'd spent away at her grandmother's house with the kids and, some strings her lawyer had pulled, her divorce was final.

Something inside of her still mourned the loss of her first love, but another part of her was anxious to turn the page on the next chapter. And true to Sebastian's word, even as her patience ran out, he wouldn't give her all of him while she was married to Luke.

He still may not touch her because she hadn't changed her name. She'd considered it, but her children carried Luke's name, and she would, too, until she married again. He would just have to deal with that. She decided there would be nothing he could do to change her mind on that point. Well, almost nothing.

Sebastian walked out of his bedroom shirtless. Sweatpants hung low on his waist. He disappeared into the kitchen and when he reappeared he carried two empty wine glasses and a bottle of red wine. She hadn't drunk it much before they'd began dating, but she loved it, especially when he drank it and she kissed him. She could taste it on his lips, his tongue. If she were being honest, it was the way she preferred her wine, on him.

He sat beside her, and she couldn't pull her eyes off his chest. Smooth. If she poured wine on his skin, she could lick it off, and nothing would interfere.

"Rumer," he said.

She dragged her eyes from his chest to his mouth. She loved the way he said her name. Nothing had changed since that first day she'd met him. The way his tongue rolled her name around like...like he was doing more than just saying her name.

"Rumer," he said it again.

She finally let her eyes meet his, and God if those soft brown eyes weren't piercing right through her like he knew every thought in her head.

"Do I have your attention?" he asked.

"You had my attention," she said as parts of her body joined in as if to say he had their attention, too.

He smiled and filled their wine glasses. "You said you had something you wanted to tell me." He handed her a glass.

Instead of telling him herself, she gave him her phone so that he could read the text for himself, while she drank from her glass.

He placed the phone on the carpet beside him, and asked, "You still have his name?"

"Sebastian"—she sipped another long gulp—"my children have his name, and he's their father."

"So, you plan to keep his name?"

"Until I marry again." She would take her "new" husband's name. Carrying her husband's name made her feel connected and part of something bigger than herself. She'd had her father's name, but it'd meant nothing. "I wouldn't want that person to think I love him less, but I want my kids to always know we'll be a family."

He glanced at her glass. "Finish it, or put it down."

The ten second warning was all she had before her back was against the cushions and he looked down at her. She wrapped her hands around his neck and pulled him down. Not kissing Sebastian was difficult. At work it was all she thought about, and she knew he knew it. Every time he could, he drew attention to his lips, his mouth.

It took no time for him to dismiss her clothes, and have her naked beneath him. He shifted and propped his arm up on an elbow and rested his head. She reached for him, not because she wanted to be covered, he told her to never be shy around him, and what seemed hard at first had become easy. She loved when his eyes caressed her body. But, he'd promised her that when her divorce became final...

"Sebastian," she hooked a finger on his sweatpants, and tugged.

He moved her hand and held it against his chest.

"Baby, I've been waiting a long time for this, too."

"Then why did you stop?"

"Because I need you to understand that you will stop carrying his name."

She stretched and angled her head so she could kiss him. "Okay," she breathed.

Returning her kiss, he took her mouth with his. Tongues wrestled. He nibbled at the corner of her mouth. He kissed her chin, and down her neck to the mound of her breasts. He used the weight of his body to push her to her back. Using one hand he cupped and massaged one breast while his other hand plumped up her other breast and held it where he wanted it allowing his tongue to play with her aching needy nipple.

At the touch of his tongue she arched her back and pushed her body up to his mouth. She'd waited for the chance to have all of him for so long. She wanted so much more. Pulling at his sweats, he stood, and let her drag them down his legs. When he went to resume his position above her, she halted him when she rose to her knees and took him into her mouth.

His gasp showed his surprise. Grabbing the back of her head with one huge hand he controlled the rhythm until she locked her hand around the base of his erection, and squeezed.

"Rumer."

She liked the way he moaned her name, so she did it again. Then she let her tongue flutter over the tip and slide down the most sensitive underside of his penis. When she slid all of him into her mouth, he increased his speed, and she couldn't do anything, but hold on. Both hands gripped the back of her head, and the full length of him filled her mouth. She placed her hands on his muscled thighs and when she felt the tension relax and felt his warmth in her mouth, she slowly withdrew him from between her lips and laid back into the cushions.

He followed her. Resting the weight of his body on his forearms, he hovered above her. Using a knee he spread her thighs.

Dropping his mouth to hers, his passion-filled kiss stoked the ache between her legs and she reached her hand between her legs. He grabbed her hand and pulled it above her head. She raised her butt off the pillow beneath it, and ground her body against his fast growing erection.

"Impatient, sweetie," he whispered against her ear.

"Yes. You promised, Sebastian." She lifted her butt again searching for the part of him that would satisfy her need.

He slid two fingers inside of her. His fingers worked her body, and it pushed her close, but it wasn't enough. She wanted him. "Sebastian." She tightened her body around his fingers. "I want you."

"Baby, I don't have any condoms," he gritted out. Then, he enclosed his mouth around one of her nipples, and sucked.

"Harder. More. Sebastian."

"Come for me, baby."

She wiggled until he let go of her nipple, and she cupped the side of his face in one hand. The strained look on his face and the tension in his body told her he wanted her as much as she needed him. "I'm on the pill—" she lost her last words as he thrust into her.

He moaned as he pushed deep into her. The sound of their bodies intoxicated her. She wrapped her legs around his back and gripped his butt with her hands. He drove deeper and with one hand cupped her chin and kissed her deep and long. She broke away for a breath, and then he took her mouth again.

He pulled away from her breaking the hold of her legs, rose to his knees, angled her body and slid impossibly deeper into her. She grabbed the cushions around her and held on as he stopped holding back his need for her. Using the thumb of one hand he massaged her clitoris, and her body exploded. When the inner muscles of her body clinched around him, his own orgasm crashed over him.

His body fell to hers, and she loved the sensation of the throb inside of her that she knew was him. As the throbs ceased, he rolled to his side. Once again propping up his arm and resting his head on a hand.

The fire that had warmed her, now seemed to hot and unnecessary. But, she loved the glow of the fire against his chest and abdomen. She traced the pattern on his skin, but the lure of kissing his chest, and letting her tongue play with his nipples couldn't be resisted.

He sucked in a breath. "Baby, wait. I need to make sure you understood me."

"Umm," she mumbled. She understood he tasted good, and she didn't want to talk.

He pinched her butt, and she glared up at him. "Hey, no fair."

"Well, you weren't listening to me." He smiled. "Your divorce is final, but you still have Luke's name." He kissed the tip of her nose. "I don't like to share."

She placed a hand on his chest. "You're not sharing me. I promise. I'm all yours." She kissed his full mouth, and wished he'd stop talking. There were so many things she wanted him to do with his mouth.

"Not now, but when you're ready...when we're ready, you won't have his name any more." He paused. "Maybe I'm okay if you hyphenate." He rolled over onto his back and pulled her on top of him. "Up," he said as he tapped her bottom.

She rose slightly, and he slid the tip of his erection into the wet softness of her body. She braced her hands on his chest and began to move. He filled her so completely.

Wait! What? Was Sebastian saying...saying he wanted to marry her? She looked into his eyes, and he smiled.

He wrapped a hand around her neck and pulled her mouth to his. "It took you long enough to understand." His kiss was a promise.

She tightened her thighs against the side of his body and she moved with him as he kissed her. As another orgasm rolled over her body, she thought this was the best ride of her life. And, in his own way, he'd just promised her forever. Forever with Sebastian. She deepened their kiss as she felt the release of his body inside of her. She wanted to have that feeling, his touch, his love for the rest of her life, and he'd just promised it to her.

She broke their kiss, and said, "I love you."

"Mi corazon, I love you."

Book Club Discussion Guide

Rumer
by Angela Kay Austin

- According to an article for the Huffington Post, nine years is the average length of a marriage in the United States. How do you think this affects men and women of various ages?

- In your experience, is marriage 'disposable' or is it becoming so, and why or why not?

- How do you think divorce affects the children of the relationship?

- Do you believe transsexuals should readily make their condition known, immediately, in relationships?

- If your spouse asked you to consider different methods of saving your marriage, due to infidelity, would you attempt it?

- Is there a line in the sand when it comes to attempting to repair a relationship? Is there a time period you would consider a limit?

- Do you think a marriage can be saved, after infidelity?

- Do you believe there are different types of infidelity? Sexual? Emotional?

- Have you ever ended a relationship because of infidelity, and then reconsidered it?

- How could Rumer have handled the situation with Sebastian differently?

More Great Books from Angela Kay Austin

 Also in Print

On the Frontline
Two terrific Angela Kay Austin Short Stories For those who serve, and the ones who love them.

Scarlet's Tears – She'd lost so very much... including her sense of self, how could she go on?

Derailed – From homeless to hopeful, this young veteran builds a life she'd thought impossible.

 Also in Print

Give Me Everything
He'd sat on top of the world... the perfect woman, a daughter, and a job that made his father proud. Now, Kendis was divorced, and his daughter wasn't really his. She'd been through the wringer in her personal life, and now LaKia thinks the only thing she can control is her career. Until Kendis. He gave her everything, and she gave it right back.

 Also in Audiobook and Print

Sweet Victory
For her employees' sakes, Victoria James quits her job to save theirs and loses the man she thought she loved. Back to Memphis, Tennessee to a forgotten relationship with her grandfather, where everything she has is stolen. Chad Kirkpatrick, her childhood love, the first man to break her heart, now a police officer, comes to her aid. Will she put her past behind her? Will Chad forgive her?

Angela Kay Austin

Bestselling author Angela Kay Austin has expressed herself through words for as long as she can remember. Poems became songs performed with her cousin at every family gathering. But, eventually, short stories filled her favorite pink diary. An infatuation with music and theater led to years playing various instruments and small extra roles in TV shows before giving way to a degree and career in radio and TV production. After completing another degree in marketing, Angela found herself combining her love for all things creative and worked for many many years in promotions and advertising. But once again, she found herself writing, which led to her first published work which stayed on her publisher's bestseller list for ten weeks. Her second release hit the bestseller list at All Romance eBooks.

She's spoken on author panels, and served on boards for various author groups. When she's not writing, you can find her reading her favorite authors, or researching her next story idea. Angela shares her downtime with her mixed-bred rescue terrier—Midnight, in the beautiful southern state of Tennessee.

She's also a member of Romance Writers of America, From the Heart Romance Writers, Chick Lit Writers of the World, and Washington DC Romance Writers.